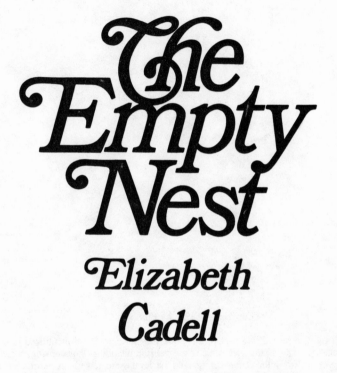

The Empty Nest

Elizabeth Cadell

William Morrow and Company, Inc.
New York

Library of Congress Catalog Card Number: 86-60043

ISBN: 0-688-06219-9

Printed in the United States of America

First U.S. Edition

1 2 3 4 5 6 7 8 9 10

1

The wedding had taken place that afternoon at the bride's home in the small town of Outercrane. Outercrane was, or had been, what it sounded: the outer part of the flourishing town of Crane. It had begun as a mere suburb, but it had something that Crane lacked – beautiful country surroundings. The houses were surrounded by woods, and there was a small modern church near the bank of the river, a pleasant park, a primary school – and Riverside House, designed and built by the father of the bride, George Deepley. Set in spacious grounds, Riverside House was large, graceful and many-windowed, with a pillared portico surmounted by a balcony, and a small, separate suite on the ground floor known as "the wing". There were two tennis courts, a swimming pool and a sauna, all of which had contributed to the popularity that the Deepley daughters had always enjoyed in the district.

The green and quiet setting of Outercrane attracted many of the old and retired people of the area; it had few shops and there was no way out of it except by the entry road, and beyond it stood woods and the bridgeless river. Crane, on the other hand, though an older town, offered much that kept its younger inhabitants from leaving in search of wider opportunities, or from commuting to London fifty miles away. Many of the younger generation stayed to become the lawyers, the doctors, the dentists and teachers of the town.

Indeed, it was the number of young people living in Crane that gave the town its bustling air. There was much for them to do there during their leisure moments, but the majority of them had formed the habit of going to Riverside House to enjoy the company of its three attractive young girls and the generous hospitality of their mother. Stella Deepley had kept open house, and nothing made her happier than to watch the comings and goings of young men and girls in every season, filling the house with chatter and cheerful sound.

There was general agreement that the wedding had been an unqualified success. Most of the guests were old friends and on easy terms with one another. The house and grounds had never looked more charming, and the food and drink had been of the high standard which had come to be expected when George and Stella Deepley entertained. The speeches had been amusing, but brief. Above all, the sun had shone, giving the reception a garden party air. Some of the conversations to be heard around the garden were not without a note of criticism, however . . .

Mrs. Russell, the wealthiest inhabitant of Outercrane and, some said, the biggest gossip, confided to her friend Mrs. Woodley that she had heard it had taken a long and hard struggle to get the bridegroom to the altar.

"Shotgun wedding, it used to be called," she said. "We all know the bride's been living with the groom for nearly a year, on and off. I've no doubt that he wanted things to go on that way."

"I wonder how they'll get along in Mozambique?" Mrs. Woodley mused. "It's not my idea of a place I'd want my daughter to go to, if I had one . . . Funny how all three of the Deepleys' daughters went so far away when they married."

"Not funny. Bad luck for George and Stella," said Mrs. Russell. "The first one in Australia, the next in New Zealand and now this last one in Mozambique. Not exactly countries that their parents can drop into for a visit. Speaking of far-flung places, where's your roving husband now?"

"Madeira," Mrs. Woodley said coldly. She did not welcome enquiries about her husband. He had retired at an early age from the Navy and now spent most of his time on

8

his yacht, sailing in warm waters. His visits to his wife were rare, and as he and she did not get on well together, fleeting. She made no secret of the fact that she was happier when he was a long way away.

She now moved with Mrs. Russell to take their places in the line that had formed to wave off the departing bride and groom. The newly-wed pair were bound for London Airport, and it had been agreed that they should go unaccompanied, the last farewells being made at the house.

"No point in driving all that way just to watch their luggage being checked in," George Deepley had said. "Let them get off quietly."

There were embraces and waving and cries of goodwill. The hired car, loaded with suitcases and the bridal couple, moved away, leaving the guests to congratulate the parents on the success of the event. George poured more champagne into glasses, put them on a tray and began to carry them round.

"All gone," Mrs. Truedom observed to Stella Deepley. "How will you and George feel, left in an empty house?"

Mrs. Truedom was a large, determined-looking widow of fifty with a loud voice and a forthright manner. On the death of her husband, she had come to live in Crane, buying a small cottage scarcely suited to her generous dimensions. The income she had inherited from her husband was adequate for her needs, but she decided to augment it. She bought a car, had a number of leaflets printed and then turned herself into a kind of Universal Aunt, fetching and carrying, shopping, taking or collecting small children from school, meeting trains, helping the meals-on-wheels organisation and also undertaking to accompany elderly travellers to stations or airports. She was too busy to make many friends, and her outspoken criticisms alienated the few she had. She considered most of the local people lacking in both energy and enterprise. For Stella Deepley she now had some advice.

9

"Now you're free," she told her, between sips of champagne. "You've got nobody to look after but yourself and your husband. Your children have all gone to the other end of the world and you're not likely to see much of them in the future – so I hope you're going to find yourself something useful to do."

"I hope so, too," Stella said, and would have said more if it had been possible, when conversing with Mrs. True-dom, to get to the end of a sentence.

"You've shown that you can run a large household, but that's all over. Now you'll have to look round for something else."

"I know. The fact is –"

"Take me, for instance. Do I sit around in my house doing nothing? No, I don't. I invented a job for myself. I'm being useful and I'm being well paid for what I do."

"That's all very well, but –"

"There are plenty of opportunities in this town for women like you to give a hand. I know you're a good cook, but you're not a good, plain cook of the kind needed in schools and other institutions. Meat and veg is all they require. Why don't you go up to London and try to get yourself into one of those specialised restaurants?"

"I don't want to –"

"Though you'd be better employed doing something to improve the lot of the needy in your own neighbourhood. There are poor people here – at least, I'm told there are. I must say most of them in these parts look pretty prosperous to me. But there are sick people, old people living alone without help of any kind. There are –"

"I know. I –"

"– opportunities all round you, opportunities for serving your fellow-men. I know of several cases – but I don't suppose this is the time or the place to tell you about them."

She moved on, half-empty glass in hand, carefully avoiding Mr. and Mrs. Harley, who were trying to waylay her.

They were a middle-aged couple who had made it their business to help all the charitable organisations of the district. Their friends had to exercise a great deal of ingenuity to escape the never-ending succession of appeals made by the pair at every encounter. Books of raffle tickets emerged from Mrs. Harley's handbag; subscription lists were produced from Mr. Harley's pockets and hopefully unfolded. The couple appealed for funds, for unwanted articles to be sold at bazaars, for outworn garments to be sent to the needy. All they asked from their friends were contributions. They were also the town's experts on how not to bring up children. They had five between the ages of six and fourteen, all of them fortunately immured in boarding schools during term time, but most unfortunately at home for holidays, free to roam the town and shatter the peace of its inhabitants. One of their favourite sports was to perform complicated manoeuvres on their bicycles on roads where traffic congestion was at its worst.

Mrs. Truedom had stopped to speak to Miss Grail.

"The third wedding in three years," she said. "It isn't many mothers who bring off a coup like that. Especially when most couples nowadays regard the wedding ceremony as superfluous. How're all your dogs?"

"They're all very well, thank you."

Miss Grail was an Honourable, daughter of a prominent politician, and regarded herself as the town's leading social light. She lived in a small house in Crane with a married couple as cook and housekeeper. Surrounding the house were several acres of rough land on which were sheds in which she bred Afghan hounds. These she took to dog shows all over England, and in her drawing room were displayed the numerous trophies they had won. She was rarely seen in anything but corduroy trousers and, even in midsummer, heavy sweaters. Today, in an old-fashioned silk dress and matching coat, she looked unfamiliar, and less impressive than usual.

"It wasn't as though any of the three girls looked like matrimonial prizes," Mrs. Truedom went on without troubling to lower her voice. "Not one of them inherited her mother's looks. Say what you like, Stella Deepley's lovely to look at. Must have been stunning when she was a girl. But all her daughters took after their father, and nobody could call him anything but downright homely. Pity the girls are to be so far away."

"A great pity . . ." Miss Grail frowned slightly. "I wonder what George and Stella are going to do all by themselves in this large house?"

"I'm waiting to see. George'll be all right. That heart attack he had a month or so ago wasn't enough to slow him down much. He's got his garden to take up a lot of his time, and his chess computer, and his war games. It's Stella who's going to find herself without a job. I've just been giving her some advice."

"Perhaps she'll get in touch with her friends again. We haven't seen much of her in the last few years."

"She's not really the social type. The only time she goes out is with George, to parties given by people they know well. Her trouble is going to be finding something she can do in her own house."

"She was always so hospitable. The house –"

"As you say, the house was always full of young people, friends of the girls. It made a lot of work for her, but she seemed to enjoy it. She had help, of course, but I never thought that woman she employed was much good."

"The work was certainly –"

"– unceasing, as I was saying. Besides all those meals for all those guests, she had the laundry to see to, and the shopping – in fact, everything."

"The girls gave her some help. They –"

"Oh, they made their beds and occasionally dusted their rooms, I'm not forgetting that. But they had none of the responsibility for the running of the house. Great mistake."

"After all those years of activity, Stella –"

"– will need something to fill her time. That's what I pointed out to her. She's an active woman. She won't be content to sit around with her hands in her lap."

"She must be able to do something more than cook."

"We'll soon find out. Or rather, she'll soon find out. She . . . Oh hello, Mr. Vernon. Enjoying yourself?"

"I would be, I would be, Mrs. Truedom, if the news of the strike wasn't so disheartening. Did you listen to the commentary on last night's television?"

"Me? No. They send me to sleep, those commentaries."

"Did *you* listen, Miss Grail?" Mr. Vernon asked her.

He was a man in his early sixties, short and stout but distinguished-looking and of a kindly disposition. He had retired from a high post in the Civil Service and was now the town's self-appointed political expert. Anybody who wanted, or did not want to be informed of the Government's latest activities had only to remain silent while Mr. Vernon explained what was being done in ministerial circles. He was also a poet; a slim volume of his verses had been published some years ago, and he had had the bitter-sweet experience of seeing them unfavourably reviewed in several leading journals. His wife had died – of boredom, some people said – shortly after he had bought an apartment in Crane. He now lived alone, but he liked dining out, and invariably invited one of the town's many widows to accompany him. One or two of them felt that they might one day be asked to fill the post left vacant by his wife.

Mrs. Truedom left him to discuss the strike with Miss Grail, and moved on to talk to Miss Minter who, elderly and self-effacing, was standing alone beside a table.

Miss Minter and her mother had once been affluent, but had lost almost all their money through following bad advice from amateur financial experts. The spacious house in which they had lived was sold, and they moved to the lower flat of a small house on the outskirts of Crane. Here they existed on their old-age pensions, supplemented by the interest on the money remaining to them. The rooms they inhabited were too small to allow them to entertain, but they received frequent visits from friends who had enjoyed their generous hospitality in the past. Miss Minter had been young enough in spirit to be included in many of the parties given by Stella's daughters.

"How their mother is going to miss those three girls," she now said sorrowfully to Mrs. Truedom.

"Yes, indeed she is. Speaking of mothers, how is yours? Isn't she here?"

"Yes. I managed to persuade her to come, and Mr. Vernon was kind enough to give us a lift in his car. She's sitting in the shade, waiting for him to take us home."

Stella Deepley, passing, stopped to say a word.

"Your glass is empty, Mrs. Truedom. Let me –"

"Don't worry about me. I'll go and get a refill," Mrs. Truedom said.

Miss Minter looked at her retreating back.

"So *efficient*," she murmured. "Always so busy, always in her car going about on all those errands." Her eyes came to rest on Stella. "She and I were saying how quiet it's going to be for you with all the girls gone."

"Yes, I suppose it will be."

"They were such a *charming* trio. And so kind. I shall miss all those delightful entertainments they used to invite me to. Still," she added, thinking of the circumstances of her own life, "you'll soon get used to being without them. One has to get used to doing without many pleasant things in life, I'm afraid."

"Yes. Your lovely house . . ."

"Oh, we're quite comfortable where we are," Miss Minter hastened to say. "All we miss – at any rate, all *I* miss is space." Her tone grew reminiscent. "I used to have a room in which I could paint. I wasn't very good, but I loved doing it. I used to lose myself for hours at a time. Now, of course,

I couldn't fit an easel into the tiny rooms we've got. So I use my spare time painting cards – Christmas cards, birthday cards, that kind of thing."

"You're quite right. One must make the most of things." Stella spoke firmly, decisively. "The girls have gone, it's true, but with Kathryn helping with the garden, George and I are going to enjoy life on our own."

Stella was forty-six, George fifty-four. They were comfortably off, and their house was the largest in the district. None of their three daughters had inherited their father's easy-going nature or their mother's good looks. All three had followed in their mother's footsteps and married early; none had possessed their mother's gift for cooking. Stella had been trained in the kitchens of famous restaurants, and her ambition had been to become a chef. But she had married instead. Now chance had taken all her daughters abroad, and Mrs. Truedom was not the only guest speculating on how she and her husband would get on in the empty house.

A year ago, George had been the senior partner of a wood-importing firm in London. He had driven every morning to Crane station and had then gone by train to the City. At weekends there had been golf, and work in his garden – a pleasant existence which had changed abruptly when he suffered a heart attack. It was not a serious one, but his doctor had told him he should retire and avoid physical strain of any kind. So George had resigned from his firm, given up golf and cut down his work in the garden.

The garden – large, and surrounding the house on all sides – was not a problem. It was in the hands of Kathryn Malden, a girl of twenty-three who had come to the town with her mother a year previously. Mrs. Malden had hoped to open a boutique in Crane, but things had not gone well, and in spite of strenuous efforts to put the shop on its feet, she had lost almost all the money she put into the venture.

She had returned to London, and now lived with an aged and ailing uncle.

But her daughter Kathryn had had enough of city life. Until the death of her father, she had lived in the country. She had recently gained a diploma at a horticultural college, and was determined to find work that would keep her in the open air. To the surprise and indignation of her mother, she decided to ask George Deepley if she could undertake the care of his garden, which she realised he could no longer manage, even with the help of a youth who did the digging. George agreed with relief and alacrity. A salary was agreed on, and he installed her in the gardener's comfortable cottage, to the satisfaction of all, except perhaps Kathryn's mother. For the reception, Kathryn had specially planted the garden with white geraniums and lily of the valley which, with the bursts of colour of tulips and forget-me-nots, had made a very pretty setting for the festivities.

The last wedding guests were leaving. A few close friends stayed on to have a celebration supper. Stella had not been content to leave the food arrangements entirely to the caterers. Cooking was still her passion, her one outstanding talent, and through the years she had enjoyed nothing so much as to find herself in her own kitchen, preparing meals for her family and their friends.

She was now completing the preparations for supper, assisted by Mrs. Preston, a woman who had been coming to work daily in the house for the past twenty years, but who was now about to retire. She was lean and leather-skinned – a widow who had come from London to Crane many years ago to join her son and daughter-in-law. Her son had died shortly after her arrival, and her daughter-in-law had departed to Vancouver in the company of a prosperous Canadian businessman. A small grandson named Kenneth had been left behind with his grandmother – for a short time only, her daughter-in-law had said on her departure. But the boy had never been sent for, and had grown up in the house his father had helped Mrs. Preston to buy. He had a free and easy, feckless outlook on life which all his grandmother's efforts had failed to change. Now, at the age of nineteen, he still lived in her house, the spare rooms of which had been rented to a succession of lodgers.

The only shop of any size in Outercrane was a grocery owned by a burly Yorkshireman named Willie Bolt. He was a widower who had two teenage daughters; Kenneth Preston was hopelessly in love with the younger of them. His first job had been in the shop, but he had been unceremoniously thrown out when his employer discovered his attachment to his younger daughter. It was difficult, however, to keep the pair apart, since Maureen Bolt worked for a hairdresser and went to the houses of clients wishing to have their hair done at home. One of these was Stella Deepley, and as Kenneth worked part-time in the Deepleys' garden, meetings between him and Maureen were easy to arrange.

Since leaving the shop, Kenneth had had several jobs, but had shown a marked talent for losing all of them. Nothing would make him stay in a job in which he felt exploited. He was a good mechanic and had worked for a time in the largest garage in Crane, but had left when a new and unfriendly foreman was appointed. Since then he had done the heavy work in George's garden, and he also worked as a waiter in a Crane restaurant.

He was a tall, thin youth with a long face that was for ever ready to break into a cheerful smile. One of his odd jobs, three years earlier, had been to help a newcomer, Christopher Hobart, to settle into the bookshop he had opened in Outercrane. This had led to Christopher's renting the two front rooms of Mrs. Preston's house. He had refurnished these and made himself comfortable, unaffected by his landlady's unceasing moans against the world and its ways, and growing to like her footloose grandson more and more. Kenneth kept him in touch with all that went on in the twin towns of Crane and Outercrane.

17

Mrs. Preston was now regaling Stella with her impressions of the wedding.

"It went off well, I'll say that for it," she observed. "Did you take a good look at what they all had on? Not a smart turn-out, I wouldn't say. Miss Minter's dress looked as if she'd washed it and it ran, and that dress and coat of Miss Grail's is the one she's trotted out for I dunno how many years. Mrs. Truedom looked all right – but did you see her knocking back the champagne? I couldn't count up." She piled plates of varying size on to a tray. "I'll miss being here, after all these years."

"And we'll miss you," Stella said.

"I've no doubt you will, in some ways. But I'm not as young as I was, and I promised meself I'd give up when I got to seventy-five, and that's what I'm doing."

"I shall keep thinking you're in this kitchen, helping me."

"It'll be different now they've all gone. I'll come in Wednesdays to do the rough, but if you want, I'll give you an extra day or two next week."

"No, thank you. I'll be able to manage."

"You should. There soon won't be all that much to do, not in the kitchen. You'll have to get busy doing something else somewhere else. You've shut yourself up for too long in this house." She took some glasses from a cupboard. "Where're you going on this holiday trip you said you was takin'?"

"Italy."

"When do you leave?"

"Second of May. I haven't told people because it wasn't certain we'd go. But now we've made up our minds."

"Well, enjoy yourselves. You deserve a good rest."

"We haven't been abroad for years. It's going to be good fun."

"I hope you'll leave that no-good grandson of mine a lot of jobs to do in the garden while you're away."

"Don't call him that, Mrs. Preston," Stella protested. "He's a nice young man."

"He's a no-good, that's what he is – a long, lazy no-good. If he'd got anything of his father in him – now, *he* was a worker. But Ken – well, look at him – in a waiter's job at that new restaurant."

"He's a good waiter. We dined there one night and he was very efficient."

"He was all dressed up and fancying himself as a future *mater dotel*. He bought that suit second-hand from Mr. Hobart."

Stella sprinkled chives on to the soup.

"How is he getting on? Christopher Hobart, I mean?"

"Him? He's a good lodger. He's quiet and he's considerate. How his bookshop's going, I couldn't tell you. People say he's doing well. Now he's opened that second-hand department. Strange he's not married. But if he was, I wouldn't be able to have them both, him and her. Not enough room. How're you going to feel, rattling around in this big house now that the last of the girls is gone?"

The supper guests asked the same question. Mrs. Russell, who owned the dress shop which had been the chief reason for Mrs. Malden's failure to set up a second one in the town, spoke frankly about the future.

"You two are going to feel lost," she said. "George'll be all right – he'll find plenty to occupy him. But how about you, Stella?"

"Stella'll be all right too," George said. "We're going to travel."

"You can't travel all the time," Mrs. Truedom pointed out. "Who's Stella going to cook for now? Toast for breakfast, salads for lunch, and a light dinner. If you take my advice, you'll sell this house and get yourselves into a nice, easy-to-run flat."

"Never." George spoke firmly. "For years, I dreamed

about this house. I planned it and I had it built the way I wanted it. And now we're going to stay in it."

The contrast between George and his wife seemed more pronounced than usual. He was a quiet, slow-thinking man with a deep sense of humour. She was quick-witted, vivacious, still extremely attractive, and in her way as generous and as warm-hearted as her husband. Self-reliant though she was, George was her mainstay, able to cope with her varying moods, her protector and adviser.

"Will you go and visit the girls?" Mrs. Russell asked.

"We will not," George answered decisively. "What, go all the way to Australia or New Zealand or Mozambique? Never. If they can get themselves here, I'll pay their fares – but Stella and I aren't going to do any long-distance trips. Just short ones."

"And no package tours," Stella said.

"No package tours," George corroborated. "I like myself to myself. No beach-and-bar sessions, either."

"We want to be free," Stella said. "I don't like herds. As a matter of fact, George and I have planned a trip and we're going off in two weeks."

"Where to?" the guests wanted to know.

"I'll give a guess." It was Kathryn Malden speaking. All heads turned to study her in her bridesmaid's outfit.

She was seated opposite her mother, who had come down from London for the wedding and had been invited to stay on for supper. Mother and daughter were outwardly alike – both were fair, slender and good-looking; both had deceptively fragile figures. But Kathryn had her dead father's level-headedness, sound common sense and calm outlook on life, while her mother was hard, ambitious and, many thought, selfish.

The greatest difference between them lay in expression. Kathryn's was a combination of the sensible and the serene. Her mother's was a mixture of dissatisfaction and petulance. Life had not brought her the luxury she craved. She had married a man without ambition, and at his death had been left with an income that was far less than she had hoped for. She had used most of her capital in the attempt to open the boutique in Crane; when it came to nothing, she decided to accept a post that had been open to her since the death of her husband: that of housekeeper to an ailing and aged uncle. She moved into his London house and used his considerable assets to engage a staff that would keep him and herself comfortable. He was now declining rapidly in health, but she knew that he had made a will leaving her all his money, and she had no reason to fear that he would revoke it.

"Well, what's your guess?" George asked Kathryn.

"Italy."

"Right. How did you figure it out?"

"Easy. You left two Italian grammars in the potting shed."

"Oh, is that where they went?"

"What part of Italy?" Mr. Vernon wanted to know.

"Naples."

"Why not Rome?"

"Stella and I saw Rome when we were young. We fancy Naples this time. I tried to get there by boat, but nothing doing. So we fly to Rome and get a connection."

"We thought it might be fun to make the connection by train," Stella said. "I've never been in an Italian train."

When the guests had done, Kathryn stayed on to help with the clearing away, and to her Stella confided more details.

"It's a sort of treat we're giving ourselves," she said. "Ever since George saw the doctor, he promised himself we'd go away for two or three weeks to get himself fit."

"Will you hire a car over there?"

"No. Taxis whenever we need them. And a really comfortable hotel." She paused. "If it hadn't been for you, we couldn't have done it."

"Why not?" Kathryn asked.

Stella looked at her with the affection that had been steadily growing since they had first met. She was, she told herself, a lovely girl. Medium height, ash-blonde hair, charming, oval face.

"Well, you're a marvellous gardener, for one thing, so George won't have to worry about his beloved plants. And you'll keep an eye on the animals, and feed them." Stella paused before continuing, "I must say, whilst I've loved looking after the girls, I'm glad that George and I are going to have the chance of being alone together. Having children is an irreplaceable experience, but they do rule your life. Now I want to spend more time with George. He's been a marvellous husband and father."

After this rather long speech, Stella smiled. "How about a husband for yourself, Katie?" she enquired, using the affectionate name both she and George called Kathryn. "He'll have to be a gardener – what would we do without you? The present candidate doesn't come into the gardening category." She hesitated. "Is there anything in it, Kathryn? I mean, is it serious?"

She was referring to Aubrey Roach, a wealthy young stockbroker who came down every weekend to Crane from his flat in London, and who spent most of his time in Kathryn's company.

Kathryn's answer came unhesitatingly.

"No," she answered calmly. "It isn't at all serious."

"But it *looks* serious, and most people think it is. He's in love with you – anyone can see that – and you appear to like him."

"Do I? Well, I like him – but that's all."

"He isn't only rich," Stella pointed out. "He's good-looking, and he's liked by almost everybody in this place. Your mother –"

"My mother hopes I'll marry him. But I won't – and that's final."

Stella closed the door of the dish-washer and turned to speak in surprise.

"You sounded as though you really meant it."

"I do mean it. But I've never said so to my mother. You're the only person I've ever told that I'll never marry him."

"He comes down here every Friday, to that cottage of his, and he stays until Monday and he sees a lot of you."

"It became a habit. I decided to break it."

"What exactly have you got against him?"

Kathryn took some time to reply. The table was cleared, the drawing room tidy, before she spoke again.

"He's too rich," she said at last. "He's got everything – looks, charm, an apartment in London, a cottage down here, a powerful car – you name it, he's got it. But he doesn't seem to me to . . . well, to spread any of it. It's all for himself. He takes me out to dinner, to lunch, on picnics, on expeditions – just ourselves, everything we want, and all the time I can't help remembering that half the world is starving or dying of disease. He doesn't seem to me to *give* anything. He makes money, and more money. At the moment he's thinking of buying a yacht. I suppose I sound ungrateful – to enjoy what he gives me and then say things against him – but I'm just trying to explain how I feel. My mother would think I was crazy if she heard me."

"She took a knock over that boutique. And she'd naturally like to see you well settled. You know, sometimes I think she might marry again. She's still young, and she's very good-looking. I shouldn't ask, but won't she have a lot of money when her uncle dies?"

"Yes. And it doesn't look as though he'll live much longer. He –"

She stopped. George, who had driven Mrs. Preston home, had returned and was standing at the kitchen door.

"Not still up at this time of night? Katie, you should have left hours ago."

"It's my fault. We've been gossiping," Stella told him.

She went up to him and put her arms round his neck. "It was a lovely wedding, wasn't it, George?"

"If you say so. My own feeling all through the ceremony was that every person in the church was fully aware that the bridegroom had at last made an honest woman of the bride. Virginal white wedding dress, my foot."

Stella made a sound of protest. Releasing him, she appealed to Kathryn.

"He shouldn't have said that, should he, Katie?"

"No, he shouldn't. For one thing –"

"For one thing," broke in George, "it makes me sound a has-been. But I've never been able to get to grips with the modern habit of anticipating or dispensing with the marriage ceremony, and I never will. Come on, Katie – I'll walk you home."

"No, thank you. I can manage to get to the cottage entirely unaided."

He looked at her in frank admiration.

"You're a lovely lass, d'you know that? I suppose you do. And in that bridesmaid's outfit, you're a stunner. You're not going to let that stockbroker fellow carry you off, are you?"

"No."

"The Lord be praised. You're too good for him. I'd rather see you with an honest, down-to-earth chap like for instance the one who owns the bookshop. Chris Hobart. I saw him giving you interested looks all through the wedding."

"He's been giving her interested looks ever since she came here," Stella said. "Katie, go home, darling." She kissed her on both cheeks. "I'll never feel all my daughters have gone while you're with us."

"That's true enough," said George.

They saw her out. George closed the front door and put out the downstairs lights.

But while Kathryn walked to the cottage, she was not thinking of herself. Her mind was on the Deepleys, and especially on Stella. The future, she thought, wasn't going to be easy for her. None of her three daughters had left Outercrane to work elsewhere. The eldest had been secretary to the local veterinary surgeon. The next had run a small language school, the third and last had worked in a florist's. None of the three had left the family home, and their mother had, through the years, been kept busy providing lunches and dinners for them and for their numerous friends. Now there would be very little cooking to do – and cooking was almost all that Stella was interested in. The house was too large for two people, but she knew that George would not sell it.

Letting herself into the cottage, she decided that there was a difficult time ahead.

Stella, undressed and in bed, was not ready to sleep. "I can't get our trip out of my mind," she told George. "It's going to be heavenly. A nice flight, a good hotel, lots of cosmopolitan people of the kind we never see here. A shimmering swimming pool and a view of Naples Bay. And all those expeditions, Pompeii and Caserta and . . . and so on. I can't wait."

"You've got to wait two weeks. I suppose you know how much it's going to cost?"

"Who cares? We can afford it. We ought to get away more often in future. This first trip is a sort of farewell to our family life, and the beginning of life on our own."

"Good. Now go to sleep."

"I'll try."

In the large front bedroom of Mrs. Preston's house, Christopher Hobart was also trying to sleep. But he was not thinking of Naples. His mind was on the wedding. More specifically, it was on Kathryn Malden, the bridesmaid with the fair hair and greenish-blue eyes. He had met her frequently at the Deepleys, and he had also met her in the town – in blue jeans, jacket or anorak, walking or cycling or driving a small, shabby car. Today, in the church, she had been standing close to him, attending the bride, and he had had difficulty in keeping his eyes off her. He had never ventured to ask her to go out with him. Her weekends were monopolised by Aubrey Roach, a man Christopher privately labelled a playboy.

It was difficult, he thought, for a bookseller and a gardener to get together. If only he sold seeds and garden implements, he would have an excuse to go and see her as she worked – among the flowers. As it was, he would have to see if he could drop in now and then and talk to her. The Deepleys wouldn't throw him out, and he might find that dropping in led to staying in. It was worth trying.

Kenneth Preston was not in bed. He was hovering in the shadows of Willie Bolt's shop. It was the only self-service shop in Outercrane, and its owner was stout, self-satisfied and prosperous. As one of his chief preoccupations was his unavailing attempt to keep his younger daughter out of Ken's reach, he would not have been pleased to know that Ken, having finished his work at the restaurant, had lured Maureen down from her room and was holding her in a close embrace. She had her father's ample proportions, so there was a great deal to hold.

"You shouldn't be here, and you know it," she said protestingly. "And I shouldn't be with you. If my father hears us, he'll come out and strangle you."

"Just let him try. If I keep this job, Maureen, he'll think more of me."

There was a wide difference in their accents. Maureen's was the Cockney spoken by the many Londoners in the district. Ken, however, had grown up with his grandmother's injunction ringing daily in his ears: "Don't you talk like me. Talk proper." He spoke with a somewhat flat local accent.

"He won't think no more of you if you keep the job for a hundred years," Maureen told him. "D'you think he's going to let me marry a waiter?"

"You love me and I love you."

"What's that got to do with it? You haven't got any money and so far you haven't managed to earn any."

"My grandmum's got money. Not a lot, but I'll get it when she's dead."

"She'll never die. Her sort don't. It's no good, Ken. You and I can talk about being in love, but that's as far as it'll ever go."

"It's gone a lot further than that, and you know it."

"Of course I know it. I must be off my head. Making hay when my father was out of the way. What I can't figure out is what'll happen if he ever finds out. Now will you push off and let me get back upstairs?"

"Mr. Hobart likes me. One day, he might give me a job. I'd like to work in his shop."

"What d'you know about books? Don't talk silly."

"When am I going to see you again?"

"Dunno. Now go away. It's after twelve."

He released her reluctantly.

"One day," he promised, "I'll have a stroke of luck, and then you and I'll get married and tell your dad to go to hell."

"Fine. Remind him to take your grandma with him."

2

The week following the wedding found Stella fully occupied with household tasks. There were the now empty rooms to be cleaned and closed. There were clothes, left behind or discarded by the last bride, to be sorted and put away or given away. The kitchen, for some time the base of catering preparations for the wedding, had to be brought back to its normal state of orderliness. Accumulated piles of used bed linen were washed and ironed and stored in cupboards. She worked busily, endeavouring to plan, as she did so, how she could best occupy her time when these tasks were done. She knew that she must look for something to fill her days; she and George were keeping only three or four rooms for their own use, and their meals would not take long to prepare. Finding her mind going round in circles, she decided to turn it to the forthcoming trip to Naples, from which she was certain she would return with clear plans for the future.

George was also looking forward to their departure, for already, so soon after the wedding, he saw that Stella was at a loss to know what to do with the hours which, when their children had been at home, had been used to the full. He was uneasy because he knew that when the present flurry of work was over, she would be forced to look elsewhere for employment.

In the past, she had done her share of social work. She had provided cakes for innumerable bazaars, she had organised most of the banquets given by the town officials. She had never been a member of any committee, but she gave help where it was needed. These interests would, he knew, continue, but they could not fill the hours she would soon be passing in the echoing house. She had never done

28

any sewing or knitting; she had no embroidery to pick up of an evening. Neither he nor she were television addicts. But she would have to find something to keep her busy.

He did his best to help her with suggestions.

"D'you ever think about taking up painting again?"

She looked doubtful.

"I haven't done any for over twenty years."

"All the more reason for getting your hand in again. You could do a portrait of me."

"I wasn't a portrait painter. All I did was seascapes – surf sweeping over rocks, waves buffeting a sea wall – that kind of thing."

"I remember a rather nice one with a couple of fishing boats."

"I was good at doing seagulls, but that's about all. Perhaps I'll buy some canvas and make a start."

"Didn't you go to a class? I remember you refusing to come out with me once because you had a painting lesson."

She laughed.

"It wasn't a class. There was a woman living near us who was quite well known as a painter – what she did mostly was murals. She saw some of the paintings I'd done and she said if I went along to her house once a week, she'd help me."

"Is there anyone round here who'd do that?"

"Nobody – as far as I know. There are people who do painting in their own homes, but I've never heard of anybody having lessons."

"Does the chap at the school – the art master – give lessons after hours?"

"No, but even if he did, I don't think I'd go. To be honest, I didn't take to him much when I met him. But speaking of painting, there's one job I'm going to tackle when we get back from Naples. Some house-painting. All the window frames could do with a facelift, and the wallpaper in our room needs changing." She paused. "That's the trouble, George. I'm only happy doing things inside the house. I've been running it for over twenty-five years. Now I suppose I've got to slow down."

"Didn't it ever occur to you that it would all come to an end when the girls went away?"

"No. I used to wonder sometimes if we had too many of their friends to stay – too many, and too often. This house became a sort of base for them all to come to on long or short visits. We very seldom had a guest room unoccupied. And there was lots of noise and movement – and happy faces."

"You certainly catered for the masses."

"Yes – and enjoyed it. But I'm beginning to realise that I shouldn't have given up all outside interests."

"You can pick them up again."

"I'm trying. But I'm not a committee woman. What I want, what I need, what I've got to have is some form of activity inside the house – something I can do which would make it come to life again. I suppose I ought to be glad that it's so peaceful, but it feels to me like a tomb. I've thought of lots of schemes – running a tea-shop or a snack-bar, but I know what your feeling is about the house. You wouldn't like it to be used in that way."

"You're right – I wouldn't. I suppose that's selfish."

"No, it isn't. It's natural. The children's friends – yes. But a commercial venture – no. I feel as you do. It's our house and I don't want it turned into a tea-shop or a restaurant."

"How do other women fill their time?"

"I don't know, but I'm going to find out."

"Knitting?"

"I often tried – it was no use."

"Sewing?"

"I loathe it."

"Making meals to send out on wheels?"

"I offered my services – they've got more women than they need."

"Cooking for people's parties?"

"There are five women doing that already."

He did not suggest gardening – he was aware that she scarcely knew one plant from another, and anything she planted put a tentative feeler above the ground, and then curled up and died. Her attempts at herb gardens had all been disasters.

Friends and neighbours called frequently, and over Stella's excellent coffee or George's high-grade whisky, put forward what they considered helpful proposals.

"What you could do," Mrs. Harley said earnestly, "is organise a central committee to collect funds for the various charities. My husband and I do what we can and people – most people – are very generous, but what's wanted – yes, thank you, I'd love another cup. You make such delicious coffee – as I was saying, what's wanted in Crane and Outercrane is a central body through which contributions to every charity can be collected. You have time on your hands now, and you would make a splendid organiser."

Miss Minter brought some of the Christmas and birthday cards she designed.

"I know you can paint," she told Stella. "All these cards are very simple to do – and you can sell them, as I do. Even if you don't need the money, the thought of earning something is very nice."

Miss Grail thought that breeding dogs was the answer to the problem.

"Pekinese," she suggested. "Small but saleable. Only trouble would be that you'd grow fond of them and you'd be sorry when you had to part with them. Give it a try."

Mr. Vernon, over a second whisky, brought out his own solution.

"What's needed in this town is a Diners' Club," he said. "You form the club, Stella – not more than twenty members

31

– and every week you provide a dinner for which all the members pay. You'll be surprised to discover that many of us here are, believe it or not, in the gourmet category."

To this suggestion Mrs. Truedom had some private comments to make to Stella.

"Scratch out gourmet," she said, "and substitute gourmand. The whole thing's an excuse for a good tuck-in."

But Stella did not want to form a Diners' Club or to breed Pekinese or paint Christmas cards or organise a central charitable committee. What she needed, she told George once again, was a job that she could do at home that would make her forget the emptiness of the rooms and the stillness of the days.

"What you need most at the moment," George told her, "is a change of surroundings. When we get back from this Naples trip, you'll find that things have straightened themselves out."

But as the days went on, he saw that she was losing some of her vivacity. She had many friends in the town, and they frequently dropped in to see her, but it was not society she needed; it was occupation.

"I want to *cook*," she told George. "I want to see the kitchen table covered with nice fresh vegetables and lovely-smelling herbs. I want to watch things sizzling on a grill. I want to make pies and pâtés – not just for a succession of guests or for old people living alone. For our family. I want . . ."

She paused, and George spoke gently.

"You want things the way they were. Well, Stella, you can't have them that way any more. The three girls have gone, and gone for good – except for the occasional visit. We're on our own. It's only natural that you should miss the girls. They –"

"But I don't."

32

"You don't what?"

"Miss them. Well, of course I miss them – but what I miss most is what went on round them. People coming and going. Voices. Movement. One of the things I enjoyed most was being able to work in the kitchen through every kind of interruption. And now . . ."

"Well yes," George admitted. "It's quiet."

"It's dead. Not a sound. Just echoes. Don't you hear them?"

"No, I can't say I do. But I can understand that you're finding it hard to adjust."

"I feel lost. Once I've written long letters to the three girls, what is there left to do?"

"It's only a matter of time before you get used to things the way they are."

"Time, yes. But while time's going on, what I want to find out is how I can keep myself busy. The housework's nothing – I can get through it standing on my head. As I told you the other day, what I want to know – what I've never had time to think about before – is how all the women I know employ their time."

"There's never been a Youth Club here," he said. "How about starting one?"

"The vicar runs a club in Crane."

"Yes, I forgot that. I suppose there wouldn't be room for two."

"No. Is it unusual, d'you think, for a woman to be so completely unable to do any . . . well, handwork? The girls used to be able to make their own dresses, don't you remember? I couldn't even sew on the buttons. Do you know that there aren't, among my possessions, any knitting needles or crochet hooks or even needles and thread?"

"What time did you ever have for sewing or knitting?"

"I had the evenings. Why didn't I get myself some embroidery and learn how to do it? Why did I let Mrs. Preston

33

do all the mending? Why didn't I join one of those commit-
tees for this or that good work?"

"Because you were busy catering for those masses."

"Yes. But looking back, it seems to me that I was in a
rut. Gold medallist housewife – and that's all."

"It was a lot. Dammit, Stella, you were doing the things
you loved doing. You ran a big show. I remember that at
the beginning, I asked you if we didn't open our doors too
widely to the children's friends."

"And I said that hospitality was my recipe for happiness.
So it was. So it still is, but I can see now that what I enjoyed
so much was the young life that went on round me. We can
still be hospitable, and I suppose we'll always welcome
friends, but cooking lunches for people like Mrs. Truedom
or Mr. Vernon or even poor little Miss Minter doesn't really
rouse me to enthusiasm."

"You sent three girls out into the world with a sound
grounding in housekeeping."

"I know. But that doesn't help me much now."

"Look, give yourself time. Let's enjoy this trip we're
going on. When we get back –"

"When we get back, I'm going to stop moaning and pull
myself together."

But before they left, she spent a morning in the town,
and returned to tell George what she had been doing.

"I've been going round talking to people," she said.

"What about?"

"I've been asking questions – some direct, some not so
direct."

"Questions about what?"

"I've been trying to find out how people fill their time.
People of so-called leisure, that is. None of them seemed to
grouse, as I've been grousing, about not having enough to
do. So I tried to discover how they kept boredom at bay."

"You found out?"

"Yes and no. Want to hear?"

"I'm listening."

"Come into the kitchen. I'll tell you over coffee."

He followed her and took a chair while she made and poured out two cups.

"Before beginning my visits," she began, "I dropped into the hospital and asked them if there was any help needed. The only thing they could think of was a librarian's job. It entailed carrying books up to each floor and wheeling them round the wards, taking away the books the patients had read and supplying them with books they hadn't read. Then downstairs, put the unwanted books back in their right places – and that was it."

"Sounds the sort of job that could be done by a ten-year-old schoolgirl."

"Quite so. So I said I'd do it. Three mornings a week, ten to eleven. Then I dropped in on the chairman of the Women's Aid Society. She said there was a lot to be done, but it was being done already. She said I could knit blankets or bedsocks, or I could go round collecting old Christmas cards for resale. I could also dress dolls, for distribution on festive occasions. All very useful, I've no doubt, but not quite what I was looking for. I went to the crèche to see if they wanted helpers. They didn't – they had a full list."

"How about a cookery school?"

"I thought of that. There are a few women who'd come, but not regularly – and I discovered that providing meals is not something anyone is anxious to do these days. The only women who seem to cook are the mothers of schoolchildren, and as far as I can gather, they sit down daily to a high tea of sausages and chips. There are bridge clubs, but I don't play. There's a writer's circle, but I don't write. Every woman I spoke to seemed to have her days filled, but I didn't come across anything interesting that I could do in my own home. My mistake has been in concentrating all my energies on one thing. But I haven't told you yet how other women spend their time."

"Go ahead."

She held up a finger.

"One: Mrs. Russell. She's got no problem about free time on her hands. She spends the morning supervising the manageress she's got in her boutique. She drives herself up to London four afternoons a week – she's got a doctor there, a dentist there and a hairdresser there. In between trips to town, she plays bridge." She held up a second finger. "Two: Mrs. Woodley. She helps every weekday morning in the Bring-and-Buy shop – no more helpers needed. The rest of the time she plays bridge, and she also teaches beginners two evenings a week."

"Three?"

"Mrs. Truedom. She's got a full-time job; you can count her out."

"Four?"

"Miss Grail. Totally taken up with her dogs."

"Five?"

"Miss Minter. Makes all the meals for herself and her mother, does all the housework and spends her free time painting those awful Christmas cards we get every year."

"Next?"

"Next and last – Mr. Vernon. He goes up to London three days a week to fraternise with his gourmet club friends. When he's not eating, he gets on with his poetry writing. Which reminds me that his poetry reading this year is on the thirty-first. We'll be back from our trip."

"Oh my God, do we have to go through another poetry-reading session?"

"Yes, we do. I can't bear to think of all those empty rows at the back."

"Mrs. Woodley won't be singing again, will she?"

"Yes. That's one of the things I like about Victor Vernon – he's too kind to hint to her that she's past it. I wish he didn't always read his own verses."

"If he didn't, nobody else would." George glanced out at

the garden. "Do you think Kathryn would like to come in and have a cup of coffee?"

He called from the window, and Kathryn came in and joined them. George went out to take her place in the garden.

"George and I have been discussing what I could find in the way of jobs," Stella said. "I wish I could have made myself useful in the garden – but I can't. You know, the first thing that put me off gardening was finding out that you have to plant things months before you need them. Another thing: when I tried planting things, they didn't appear – they disappeared. Perhaps I put them in upside down, so that they're finding strange plants springing up in Australia. Even my herb gardens died on me. A pity, because I love herbs so much when they're in a kitchen. I used to stand entranced by the beauty of the vegetables and herbs I was using. Isn't nature wonderful? Just think how perfect a bunch of grapes looks, the lovely red roundness of a humble tomato. And the way a bean nestles in its soft pod-bed, and the perfect order of peas in their shells. Some people call cooking an art; others call it a science. Myself, I call it a feast for the senses."

Kathryn looked at her with affection. Lovely skin, soft, lustrous, wavy dark hair, large dark eyes. A kind, energetic, intelligent woman temporarily at a loss to find something that would fill the empty hours of her life.

"It's curious," she remarked, "that some women do nothing at all, but never feel unoccupied."

"That came up when I was talking to George just now. How can they feel unoccupied? Hairdressers and dressmakers and bridge sessions and visits to London and visits to their chums and – for those who want it – television round the clock."

Kathryn laughed, finished her coffee and rose.

"What I really came in for," she said, "was not to have coffee, but to say I'm going into town to the bookshop. I ordered a book and it ought to have arrived by now. I also want some seeds. Want anything while I'm there?"

"No thanks. Are you taking your car?"

"The bathtub? No. I'll go on my bike."

She set out. The seed-buying did not take long. Then she made her way to the bookshop from which, three years ago, the old sign had been removed and replaced by another – *Christopher Hobart Books Old & New*.

Going in, she asked for and got the book she had ordered. Walking round a shelf on her way to the cash desk, she ran into a high aluminium ladder. Christopher Hobart was standing on the top rung. The ladder swayed, and the armful of books he was carrying came down in a cascade on to Kathryn's head. She put up her arms to shield herself from the avalanche, and saw Christopher standing before her.

"I'm most awfully sorry," he said in a tone of remorse. "Are you hurt?"

She shook her head.

"I don't think so. What a silly place to put a ladder!"

"Yes, it was."

"But it was my fault, I suppose; I walked into it."

"Are you sure you're not hurt?" He was pale with concern.

"Quite sure, thanks."

His assistant had come up and was picking up the books from the floor.

"Not that one," Kathryn said. "I've just bought that."

Christopher took it, wrapped it, accepted the money and gave her the change.

"I haven't seen you since the Deepley wedding," he said. "May I say that the bridesmaid's dress was a great success? It was the first time –"

"– you'd seen me dressed up."

She was going to the door.

"I'll look in and see how you are," he said.

"You think I might have delayed concussion?" she enquired.

38

"It's possible."

"Come whenever you want to. I'm always in the garden. Goodbye."

She had gone, and he was left unsatisfied. She wasn't always in the garden. There was that chap Roach, who came down every weekend and monopolised all her free time. She went out with him, she dined and danced with him; in the opinion of the inhabitants of Outercrane, she was all but engaged to him. Much of this information had come from Kenneth.

"He's been after her for a long time," he had told Christopher. "Proper show-off, he is. Man, you should see what he wears – the kind of clothes you see in those adverts – you know the sort of thing? Old country mansion, car with chauffeur, and this chap looking down his nose, dressed in the latest à-la-mode. Myself, I don't go for him. Not my type. But most people think he gives tone to the town. I dunno why she doesn't marry him."

"Does he know many people here?"

"He knows a lot of them – but he keeps himself to himself, mostly. Katie's the only one he spends time with."

If her weekends weren't free, Christopher argued to himself, he might be able to get a word or two with her during the week. She had said that she was always in the garden. He could pretend he wanted some cuttings – something of that kind; any excuse would do; anything that would enable him to see her again . . .

For seeing her again, he realised with mingled elation and foreboding, was now the prime objective of his existence.

3

The trip to Naples began auspiciously. The day was fine, with a slight but bracing breeze. A recent shower had left the garden looking its loveliest: the house seemed to be telling them to enjoy themselves and come back soon.

George and Stella said goodbye to Kathryn, left the house keys with her and took their places in George's capacious car, in which Ken was driving them to the airport. George was in a grey suit; Stella had bought a summer outfit which she considered just the thing for a sojourn in a warm city. She had pinned on to it – against George's advice – her one valuable piece of jewellery – a brooch known as Aunt Mary's crown, an heirloom which as a rule was kept in George's safe behind the reproduction Matisse on his dressing-room wall.

The London streets seemed less crowded than usual. Ken, a skilful driver, got them to the airport in good time, and there he left them.

"Now we're really on our own," Stella said, watching George load suitcases on to a trolley. "Let's check the baggage and get into the departure lounge and take a look at the duty-free."

The departure lounge was scarcely less full than the arrival hall. Chief among the groups assembled were about a dozen casually attired travellers wearing labels marked "Juniper Hotel, Naples".

"That's where we're going," Stella said with something less than pleasure. "I didn't think it was a hotel that took package tourists."

"All hotels take package tourists," George told her.

"Well, that group will probably go on to Naples by plane. We'll have a nice train ride."

On arrival at Rome they made the connection from the airport to the station in a taxi, ignoring the buses that made frequent trips to and fro. Rome was sunny; the buildings looked attractive and well cared for. Their spirits were high. Here they were, a well-turned-out English couple ready to see the sights of Naples and go back to recount their adventures to all their friends.

They met their first set-back at the station. They had been told that porters were scarce, but George had no sooner uttered one of his few words of Italian – *facchino* – than several shabbily garbed men leapt from nowhere and surrounded them. There was a good deal of shouting, some pushing, and then one of the men succeeded in thrusting the others out of the way.

"I spik Inglese," he informed George and Stella. "I take you to train. Where you go?"

"Naples," said George.

"Ah. Napoli." The man picked up a suitcase in each hand, balanced a third on his shoulder and gave the last one – the heaviest – to George.

"You take heem," he ordered. "Come. First class?"

"Yes," said Stella.

They followed him. They already had their tickets and reservations for the journey. The platform seemed a long way away, and when they went through the barrier, they found themselves being led down one which seemed endless.

"First class is top side," the porter informed them.

Top side meant almost the end of the platform. George put down the suitcase he was carrying with a sigh of relief. The porter dropped the others and came close to George and Stella.

"You must listen to me," he said. "You are going to be robbed. In Napoli, everything will be robbed from you." He pointed to Stella's brooch. "Take heem off."

She hesitated, and he became insistent.

"Off, off, off. And your wallet – where is he?" he asked George. "Put heem in your pocket inside, and your bag" – he pointed to Stella's handbag – "they will rob heem too. Never, never must you take a bag in this way. You must put heem round your neck – so. The people in Napoli – they will snatch. Everybody knows that they are snatchers. I am telling you this so you will know when you are there. Even your watch they will snatch from you. So remember what I am saying."

The part of the platform which had seemed so empty when they first reached it was now becoming uncomfortably crowded.

"Lotsa people," the porter said unnecessarily. "When train come, you follow close to me. Give me my money now – it will not be possible when the train comes."

They soon learned why. The train for Naples came in with its corridors crammed with those wishing to disembark. As it drew to a stop, the travellers on the platform made a concerted rush to get on board.

"Keep close, keep close," shouted the porter.

He had grasped the door of a carriage and was being dragged the last few yards.

"You stay here," he shouted to Stella. "Your husband, he come with me. Keep one suitcase with you, but watch heem with all your eyes."

Stella stopped beside a suitcase. The porter fought his way through the disembarking crowd, using the three suitcases as battering rams. Down the corridor he and George fought their way, until the porter spied an empty seat in an otherwise full compartment. He went in and dropped a suitcase on to it and then told George to put the others on the rack and keep the seat while he went back to fetch Stella. She appeared with him when George had given up all hope of ever seeing her again. She took the seat and watched the porter fighting to get down the corridor and out of the train before it began to move. They caught sight of him trapped in a crowd on the platform – but he had been paid.

"Overpaid," George said grimly from his half share of Stella's seat. "A golden shower, it was."

Stella had recovered her breath.

"He deserved it," she said. "How would we ever have got on without him?"

The train was gathering speed. Every compartment was full, the corridor so crowded that it was almost impossible to walk along it.

"So much for reserved seats, first class," George said. "But we're on, and as you said, we couldn't have got on if that porter hadn't got us on."

Stella was adjusting her suit, which had suffered from being dragged through the crowd.

"He was right about the snatching," George said. "I was told by someone who'd lived in Naples – anything they can snatch, they snatch. They open car doors at red lights and grab women's bags off their laps. And one fellow had his wrist-watch pulled off when he was backing his car into his own garage."

"We'll be all right at the hotel," Stella reassured him.

Sharing the compartment with them were three Italian nuns and a German couple, who, after a brief greeting, sat throughout the journey without uttering a word. The train was an express, and they drew into Naples just over two hours after leaving Rome. They had no trouble finding a taxi, and the hotel, when they reached it, looked the kind that Stella had been hoping for – a reassuring cross between the comfortable and the luxurious. When they had checked in, they found a platoon of small, uniformed pages waiting to carry their luggage up to their room. Soon they were unpacking. It was close on seven o'clock.

"A drink is what I need," George said longingly. "Let's find a bar. I don't suppose dinner'll start before eight – that'll give me time to get over that hellish train ride."

They had baths, and George changed his suit while Stella put on a dress which the London shop assistant had called an attractive little number. She replaced Aunt Mary's crown; then, feeling relaxed and pleasantly expectant, she accompanied George to the bar.

It was empty, except for a somewhat surly barman. It remained empty until the time came for them to make their way to the dining room.

"When we find our feet, we'll try dining out," George said. "But not until I've got together a few more words of Italian."

The dining room was half empty until there trooped in the travellers George and Stella had seen at London airport. They were wearing T-shirts and, in most cases, jeans, and Stella began to feel overdressed. There was much laughter from the adjoining tables, loud jokes and teasing exchanges, but nobody so much as glanced at George and Stella.

They had coffee in the residents' lounge. The package tourers passed them on their way to board a bus for a night tour of Naples. There seemed nothing to do but tell themselves that they were tired, and go up to their room. Here Stella spread out the list she had compiled of the expeditions they planned to make.

"Pompeii tomorrow," she said.

"With comfortable shoes," George warned. "There's a hell of a lot of walking to do there."

They went the next morning by taxi to Garibaldi station and embarked on a local underground train which took them, making about fifteen stops on the way, to Pompeii Scavi. Here they got off and walked to the entrance, together with hordes of other tourists. They came to what they thought was a ticket office, and queued up with a number of foreigners, only to be told by the ticket collector to go another fifty yards away in order to buy their tickets.

"Two long queues and we're not even in yet," George remarked. "And I'm roasting. Not a bit of shade to be seen."

They were in, after negotiating a short, steep rise. Before them was a long excavated street. At the end of this they came to the Forum, and Stella took out her guide book. To both of them it began to seem that they were back in Roman days. They walked along street after well-preserved street, too fascinated by what they were seeing to notice the distance they were covering.

They came to a restaurant, but it was full and suffocatingly hot. They unpacked the sandwiches the hotel had provided and ate them as they walked among the ruins.

They had arrived at about eleven. They left at four, hot, exhausted, with much ground still to be covered, but carrying with them indelible impressions of what they had seen.

There was no visit to the bar that evening. They had drinks in their room while easing their aching feet.

"We'll feel more rested tomorrow," Stella said. "I hope."

"What's for tomorrow?" George asked.

"Capri. It'll be lovely."

It was certainly lovely. They enjoyed the boat trip but were dismayed to find the island so crowded with tourists that it was impossible to find a place in which they could sit down. They went in a funicular up to the main town – a two-minute journey – and found themselves in the miniature main square, where chairs and tables were placed outside a number of cafés. Every table and every chair was occupied, some by the now familiar package tourists from London.

It was slightly less crowded at Anacapri. They had not brought food with them. They found a café and had their first local pizza. Then they went to the top of the island by chair lift. Here there was a stupendous view of the whole Bay of Naples. There was also, to George's relief, a shaded café in which he bought the celebrated local ice-cream for himself and Stella.

They left the island with regret on the six thirty boat, once again footsore but not in the state of exhaustion they had been on the previous day.

"All the same, I'd give a lot to have a quiet day tomorrow," George said yearningly.

"Tomorrow's the archaeological museum."

"I know, I know. But it'll still be there if we don't go to it until the day after tomorrow."

"And then there's Herculaneum and Vesuvius. And Ischia."

"And Paestum and Báia. And what's left of Pozzuoli, and Sorrento. Then what's left of us goes home."

The sights were interesting, impressive, riveting. But apart from sightseeing, no new interest entered their lives. They passed and repassed the package tourists and other people they recognised as fellow-guests in the hotel – but not one gave a smile or a nod or any other indication of their existence.

"We wanted to be on our own," George said, "but I did think we'd be able to exchange a word or two with someone now and then. And all those dresses you bought – I haven't seen any other decently dressed women since we've been here."

"Perhaps it's our fault. We've expected people to be friendly, and so they are – within their own group. There might be something to be said for package tours, after all."

"There must be a happy medium. Out in the cold, like us, or constantly surrounded, like them. I must say I prefer to do our sightseeing on our own."

"So do I. Though I'd sometimes like a guide. Reading it all up seems to me to be learning the hard way."

Stella, too, was feeling a sense of isolation, but she would not admit it. She was getting tired – tired of sightseeing, of

46

walking, of meals alone with George while all around them were revellers.

And then, at the beginning of their second week, something happened to change the situation. As Stella walked away from the reception desk after asking for her door key, she was stopped by a man of about George's age – tall, slightly bald, his manner and bearing that of a cultured man of the world.

"Forgive me," he said, "but I just heard the reception clerk mention your name, and I wondered . . . are you by any chance one of the Deepleys from a place called Crane in Middlesex?"

"Yes," Stella smiled. "I'm surprised you've heard of it. Most people haven't. Do you know it well?"

"I lived there as a boy," he told her. "I –"

He stopped. George had joined them. Stella began an introduction, but the stranger concluded it.

"My name's Anvil," he told them. "Oliver Anvil. Perhaps you know of my grandfather, who had a house in Crane until he died. I lived with him until I was nine."

"Of course we've heard of him," George said. "He used to open his gardens to the public once a month. He was the first in Crane to do it. He also had a small menagerie of some kind."

Oliver Anvil motioned them to a sofa.

"Could you spare a moment to talk?" he asked. "It's an immense pleasure to remember Crane. I was very happy there."

"We're actually from Outercrane," Stella told him. "My husband built a house on ground that once belonged to your grandfather. They used to call it Anvil Woods."

It was the beginning of a pleasant and profitable association. Oliver Anvil was not staying at the hotel – he was, he said, staying with friends in the town. But he found time to drop into the hotel every morning to see George and Stella; he took them in his car on expeditions and proved to be interesting and informative in all the places they visited. They went with him to Báia and Cumae; they dined in restaurants into which tourists never found their way. His Italian was fluent, his knowledge of Naples wide and detailed. The pleasure they took in his company was not lessened by the quiet, unobtrusive attention he paid to Stella. This, she felt, was an unexpected bonus to the pleasant anticipation with which she and George had looked forward to the trip.

"What a difference it's made, knowing somebody like him to go around with," she remarked to George. She had completely recovered from her fatigue. "He's nice, isn't he? D'you like him?"

It would have been difficult not to like him. He was a quiet man, handsome, well-informed and world-travelled, with a fund of local knowledge which he took pleasure in passing on to George and Stella. He spent a good deal of time with them, showing them the old part of the city and telling them its history. But as the days went by, Stella felt that she could have done with less detailed history. It was tiring enough to walk through the vast rooms of the Caserta Palace without having to learn about Bourbon kings. It was difficult to take in facts regarding Ferdinand II and the inauguration of a railway to be built to the Palace. Anecdotes were interesting, but she found them difficult to retain in her mind.

"Ferdinand II died here at Caserta," Oliver Anvil told her and George. "The queen never left the sickroom. He was only forty-nine when he died – it seems very young to our minds, doesn't it? It's a curious fact that although he was in a terribly emaciated condition at his death, the queen had his portrait painted by a man named Domenico Coldara, and distributed twelve copies of the portrait among the courtiers. Not a very happy memento, I would have said."

Stella agreed. In her head she was accumulating a jumble of names and dates, which she tried in vain to sort out. She was proud of George's ability to take in all he was told, but for her part, saturation point had been reached.

It was a relief to go on expeditions up the Amalfi coast. She insisted on sitting at the back of the car, while George sat beside Oliver Anvil and listened to the stream of facts that flowed effortlessly from his lips. Stella allowed her mind to stray to the torrent of traffic through which the driver made his expert way. From time to time, items of history floated back to her – the account of the hermit pope and his renunciation of the papal throne:

"We have Petrarch's word that although the pope took the papal chair unwillingly, he left it with pleasure."

"It must have been an astonishing scene," George remarked.

"Yes, it must," said Stella, and wished Oliver Anvil would speak less of popes and more about Emma Hamilton. But about this famous figure, he had little to say.

"It's extraordinary," he said, "that Sir William Hamilton is best remembered today because he married Emma Hart. In point of fact, he was a very distinguished figure in Naples on his own account. He was a successful diplomat and had an international reputation as an antiquarian and he made himself known, too, because of his observation of Vesuvius. For thirty-six years he was British Minister, and was extremely popular. He wrote of the eruption of the volcano in 1767, when he decided it was time to leave his villa, and went to Portici Palace to warn the king that he should leave the neighbourhood. This, by the way, was Ferdinand IV. But by the time the court left the palace, the lava had covered three miles of the road along which they were travelling. There was general panic in Naples that night, as you can imagine. The churches were opened and people moved through the streets carrying saints in procession. Two days afterwards – this, I think, was October twenty-second – there was a terrifying noise from the volcano. Ashes and cinders came down in showers. The decks of ships at sea became covered with them. In time, the mob forced the Cardinal to bring out the head of St. Januarius. It was taken in procession to the Ponte Maddalena – that's the part of the city nearest to Vesuvius. Contemporary witnesses assert that the volcano quietened down the moment the Saint caught sight of the mountain."

Stella nodded. Her brain, she admitted to herself, was not up to all this. She felt that she could have written no more than two lines of an essay on all that Mr. Anvil had told them.

"Goethe," he proceeded, "left an interesting account of his visit to the Hamiltons. He called Sir William a man of the most consummate taste. He also got a look at Sir William's secret storehouse, crammed with treasures – busts, bronzes, candelabra – all bought over the years, all splendid, all extremely valuable."

"Lady Hamilton –" began Stella.

"He had a Greek dress made for her. She wore it when she gave her exhibitions. Goethe spent two evenings among her audience – his impressions are given in his *Italian Journey*."

That was all very well, Stella thought, but if Emma's looks were all they were said to be, Goethe would have written less about the Greek dress and more about what was underneath it. He had had, after all, two evenings in which to gather impressions.

"Goethe also spoke of the Hamiltons going to meet Nelson when he came in with the fleet," said Oliver Anvil. "Lady Hamilton had been ill, and fainted at the sight of Nelson."

"One of her 'attitudes', perhaps?" Stella suggested.

To George, in their hotel room, she reported that her brain had ceased to function.

"How much of what you've been listening to have you really taken in?" she asked him.

"I've enjoyed most of it. He certainly goes into a lot of

detail. Except about himself. I haven't managed to find out much about him. Have you?"

"Well, I know he was living in a house in Bath, but his lease is up and he's got to move – he doesn't yet know where. I invited him to look us up. Aren't you longing to get home? I am."

But before they left Naples, an unpleasant event marred the end of their holiday. They returned from a short shopping expedition on their last-but-one morning to find that the door leading to their balcony was open, and several small articles were missing from among their possessions.

"My alarm clock," George said furiously. "And that silver box of yours that you keep your –"

"Oh, George – Aunt Mary's crown!" Stella cried. "It's gone! Gone!"

It had indeed gone. Oliver Anvil, coming for his usual morning visit, found a gloomy George and a distraught Stella.

"We were only out for just over an hour," she told him. "And as you know, our room's on the fourth floor. Nobody could have climbed up. They must have got over the division from one of the balconies on either side of us."

"You've informed the police, of course?" Oliver asked.

"We informed the management. They've got it all in hand," George told him.

"Did anyone else lose anything?"

"Yes," said Stella. "Two American women and a Swedish couple lost some jewellery. Nothing valuable. The only good thing was the brooch I've lost – it was left to me by an aunt, and it was worth a good deal of money. I wish to heaven I'd taken George's advice and left it at home."

"So do I," said Oliver. "You're not likely to get it back. I'm sorry about it – it's spoiled your trip."

He was right on both counts. No hope of recovery was given by the police, and the robbery of her most – her only – expensive piece of jewellery darkened Stella's outlook.

Even George's reminder that the brooch had been well insured could not console her for its loss.

Oliver Anvil was sympathetic, but not as helpful as she had hoped he would be. It was no comfort to learn that a king – his name escaped her – had once had to apply to the King of Thieves in order to have some stolen articles restored to two of his guests. What she needed was someone who would get something more than vague reassurances out of the police.

Oliver saw them off. They abandoned their train return tickets and went by air to Rome. He promised to visit them in Crane, and left them with a feeling that they had made a charming and interesting friend, and a hope that he would keep his promise and pay them a visit.

4

On her return from Naples, Stella wasted no time in putting her new energy to use. She drove first to the hospital to inspect the books she was to distribute. Some of them were in bad condition; others treated of themes she considered far too violent to be read by convalescents. After sorting them, she went to Christopher Hobart's bookshop and bought replacements.

Her next visit was to Crane, where she bought paint and brushes and wallpaper. With these she returned home and set about decorating the house. She began with the hall.

"Want any help?" George enquired, watching her saturate a roller with paint.

"No, thanks. I've got more spare time than you have – and what's more, I'll enjoy doing it. You wouldn't."

"You could give the job over to the professionals."

"Why? I've done it before, and I did it well. You can help Katie and Ken in the garden."

"They seem to have got some extra help. Haven't you noticed?"

"Noticed what?"

"The presence of Christopher Hobart among the flowers."

"I know that he came into the garden to talk to Katie. I saw him from the window."

"You've got your tenses wrong. He *comes* into the garden to talk to Katie."

Stella, up a ladder, looked down at him in surprise.

"You mean he's making a habit of it?"

"If every morning comes under the heading of a habit, then yes, he's making a habit of it."

"Every day?"

53

"Every single morning."

"Anything in it, do you think?" Stella asked hopefully.

"It's anybody's guess. From what I've seen, she doesn't seem to be encouraging him."

"He never showed much interest in her before."

"I suppose Roach was in the way. It was the bridesmaid's dress that stirred him into action. Incidentally, I've noted a falling-off in her weekend engagements with Roach."

Stella drew the roller down the wall.

"I'm looking forward to the time when she drops him altogether," she said.

"Her mother would have something to say about that."

"Nothing her mother says has much effect on Katie."

"But her mother says it all the same."

"She doesn't do it out of motherly love. I think she wants to see Katie married to someone with money – to ease her own conscience."

"What's her conscience got to do with it?"

"Work it out for yourself. The only money Katie's got, besides what she earns here, is the small amount her father left her. Her mother has always had a certain amount of money of her own, but I don't think she's ever given any of it to Katie. When her mother comes into her uncle's money, she'll probably keep that for herself too. So that's why she's interested in seeing Katie comfortably settled. She won't look kindly on Christopher Hobart – if he ever comes into the picture."

"He's doing his best. He looks to me the kind that can take a lot of discouraging."

"Well, I wish him luck."

"So do I. He'll need it. She could do a lot worse. He's a nice fellow, and he's got a modestly flourishing business. But not a tenth of Roach's assets."

Stella came down the ladder for some more paint.

"I hope Christopher can win her round," she said.

54

"If he does, there goes our gardener. Speaking of gardeners – if Ken comes under that heading – he's lost his job."

Stella stared at him uncomprehendingly.

"Lost his job?" she echoed. "You don't mean he's been thrown out again?"

"Out of the restaurant – yes."

"But why?"

"He says he sacked himself – but he also admits that the management didn't like his fraternising with the customers."

"But when we dined there, he was –"

"– on his best behaviour."

"When did you hear this?"

"He told me this morning. He's out in the garden now, digging."

"Is he upset?"

George laughed.

"Upset? He's happy because he didn't much like the job."

"If he's not careful, he'll soon find that nobody in this town will take him on."

"Would you think me crazy if I did?"

She was half-way up the ladder again. She turned her head.

"If you did what?" she enquired.

"If I took him on for the summer. There's a hell of a lot to be done, and not only in the garden. There are plenty of odd jobs here in the house. He's a good handyman. Katie's got her hands full and so have I. I'd like to keep him on for a few months, full time. What do you think?"

She stopped work and gave the matter some consideration.

"It's a good idea," she said at last. "It helps him, and it helps us. Put it to him and see what he says. Why not go and ask him now?"

"I won't have to." George gestured towards the window. "He's on his way here."

They stood together at the open window and watched him approach.

"Whistling," George remarked. "That answers your question about whether he's upset."

Ken drew nearer. The first thing about him that strangers noted was his size. He was tall, but his shoulders were so wide that they gave him a square look. His feet were large and so were his hands. He moved slowly, with something of a sailor's gait. Seeing George and Stella at the window, he stopped whistling, and addressed them.

"Did you tell her the good news, Mr. Deepley?" he asked George.

"Yes, just a moment ago," George answered.

"My grandmum's upset. When I say upset, what I mean is she's on the boil."

"I don't wonder. You're certainly good at chucking away jobs," George told him. "Got anything else in mind?"

"Haven't had time to think," Ken answered. "It happened kind of sudden, last night. They handed me two weeks' pay and said 'That's it'. I asked them what I'd done wrong, and they said I was there to serve, not to socialise. Where's the harm in chatting up the customers while they chew?"

"It's unprofessional," said Stella. "What do you propose to do with yourself now?"

"What they say actresses do – rest."

"Mr. Deepley's got a proposal to make. Want to hear it?"

"If you've got any job ideas, spill 'em. I'm not promising to go after 'em, mind you. When I've just left a job, I get a nice free feeling. I pretend I'm one of those guys who have enough dough to keep their noses well away from the grindstone. Have you heard of anything that's going?"

"No. But it occurred to me," George told him, "that for the next few months the garden is going to need more hands than Katie's and mine and your part-time contribution. If you want to sign on full time until October, it would take a weight off my mind."

Ken's countenance brightened.

"You mean work in the garden with you 'n Katie?"

"Yes. Work. W-o-r-k. If you slacken off, you'll get the sack. Is that understood?"

"That sure is understood. Mr. Deepley, sir, you're a real friend."

"I was. Now I'm an employer. Do you want the job?"

"Do little chicks cheep? Show me the dotted line and I'll put my thumb print on it."

"Come inside, and we'll discuss it," said George.

Stella took off her paint-splashed overall and strolled outside to talk to Kathryn. She found her cutting flowers for the house.

"Do you know Ken has got the sack from that restaurant he was working in?" she asked her.

"Yes. He told me when he arrived this morning. I said bad luck, but he said no luck was bad when it turned a slave into a free man. Couldn't you apply the word incorrigible to someone like him?"

"Yes. Incorrigible or not, George has taken him on as an extra hand for the summer. Full time."

Kathryn's eyes widened. Then she gave a sigh of relief.

"I'm glad," she said. "There's an awful lot to be done here in the spring and summer. Sometimes I find myself doing more than I want to, because I'm afraid to let George do too much."

"And George is frightened that *you*'ll do too much."

Kathryn laughed. She moved to another flower-bed; Stella followed her and sat on a low wall.

"How's the house-painting going?" Kathryn asked.

"I'm enjoying it. If you want the truth, I'm dreading the time I'll have got through it. But I've made up my mind that I'm going to stop thinking about what's gone, and find

57

myself something useful to do. My cooking days appear to be over."

Kathryn looked at her with compassion. She knew that it would not be easy for her to find occupation or interest to fill her days. She was not merely a good cook. There were nowadays countless women who could turn out meals of good quality. It had become almost routine to invite guests to food of international flavour. There were Chinese dinners, curry dinners; there were pizzas and paellas, there were wine and cheese gatherings. Hostesses spoke glibly of the merits of tandoori chicken, or discussed the best way of treating gnocchi. Steaks were served in a dozen different ways. But Stella's skill surmounted these dishes. Her cooking was of the kind that earned high praise not only in England but also on the Continent, the kind that sent travellers miles out of their way to eat at famous restaurants. She was a culinary artist, using and mixing ingredients as painters used and mixed colours.

"Where," Kathryn asked her, "did you first learn to cook?"

Stella left the wall and balanced herself on the side of a wheelbarrow.

"Where? It was more a case of when than where. My parents took me with them on a trip to France. I was about twelve. There was a mix-up at one of the hotels we'd booked rooms at, and we were put into an annexe. My room overlooked the kitchens, and I had a good view of what went on when they were preparing the meals. Gradually, I became interested, and then fascinated. We stayed there for ten days, but before the first week was over, I'd found my way into the kitchens as a spectator. I just stared – and stared. I never got in the way, but I watched all the various cooks at their various jobs – sauce-makers, bread-makers – and I saw the food that was bought and how they dealt with it. My parents thought I was crazy – I was supposed to be sunning myself on a beach."

"And then?"

"And then I got permission from my parents to take lessons in cooking. It was a struggle – a fight – to get them to give in. Their argument was that I could take up music, at which I wasn't bad – and painting, at which I was a bit over average. They couldn't picture me as a cook. But at last I got my way. I began to take lessons in cooking, first in London and then in Paris. I was a sort of apprentice under a succession of chefs, some of them famous. By the time I met George, I was at the banquet stage – in other words, pretty high in the profession. He'd never met a girl whose ambition it was to become a chef. I made it clear to him that I was a career woman – but that didn't worry him. Then I fell in love with him and I forgot about the career and we got married and he brought me to this house and soon I found myself cooking for a growing family. Which is what I've done for the past twenty-five or so years. That's what millions of other mothers did, but they didn't make their kitchens the centre of their interest. I did. That was my big mistake. For years, I was on call all round Crane for any charitable parties where food was being provided. I didn't do all the top-level dishes I'd been trained to make, but I set a high standard for my family. I taught them to *respect* food. There were no refrigerator meals in our house when the girls were young. We ate regular meals round the dining table."

"Did the girls do much cooking?"

"They were taught by me, but none of the three was ever interested in actually producing meals. And looking back, it seems to me that I was crazy to confine myself to that sole talent. I should have seen things more in proportion. But I hadn't much housework to do – the girls did their own rooms, Mrs. Preston took care of the rest of the house. My job was in the kitchen. There were other things to do, of course – shopping for the children's clothes when they were young, driving them to and from school until they were able

59

to go on their own, paying the household bills, keeping the household accounts. But it all began to lessen as first one daughter and then another got married and went away. With the three of them gone, *everything* seems to have gone."

"I feel sorry," Kathryn said, "that none of them stayed in this country. It would have been fun for you to help them into their new homes –"

"– and give them some furniture and fix curtains and carpets and kitchen equipment – and then sit back and wait for the babies to arrive." Stella sighed. "Yes, it would have been fun."

"Didn't you ever want to learn to grow things? Herbs, vegetables . . ."

"Yes. But I hadn't any idea of how to be a gardener, and George took care of that side of things. He tried to teach me, but I've told you before that I was no use in a kitchen garden – or any other garden. Now I come to mention it, I'm not much use anywhere."

"That's nonsense."

"Not really. Listening to that man we met in Naples – Oliver Anvil – I felt depressed – deflated – because I realised how little I knew. People told me for years that I was crazy to limit myself to my kitchen, but at least in it I was competent. Now I feel lost, and not only because my job's gone. What I can't get used to is the way things are changing, leaving me feeling like a dodo. Take electronics. Do you know anything about electronics?"

"No."

"Neither do I. But your children will. I use a calculator to add up my household accounts, but I haven't the first idea what makes it function. Yet children use computers nowadays. Schools teach with computers. I used to play noughts and crosses on paper, but your children will play noughts and crosses on computers."

"They may use them as you use a calculator for doing your accounts. But they won't necessarily understand them."

"Oh yes, they will. Children don't even need to learn their multiplication tables any more. They're growing up watching spacecraft in orbit, and they know what makes them go round." She went back to sit on the wall. "I'm a long way off sixty, but I know it's too late for me to catch up. I'm living in a world which I don't understand any more – and when you look at it that way, my gropings to find myself a new job or jobs seem rather small change." Once more she sighed. "Tell me, Kathryn – is it too late for me to take up sewing?"

"But you hate it."

"I wouldn't mind doing one of those tapestries that do all the groundwork for you, so's all you have to do is follow the lines and choose the right colours. Surely any fool can do that?" She paused. "One of my troubles, Katie, is that I like my friends, but I'm not keen on spending much time with them. It all seems so pointless, this meeting for morning coffee and a chat, and going out to tea for another chat, and going to cocktail parties where you're crammed into a room with too many people, all shrieking to make themselves heard. I do it sometimes, but I come away feeling it's all been the most awful waste of time."

They moved together to a rose-bed. Before picking the roses, Kathryn drew on protective gardening gloves.

"You've never told me much about your Naples trip," she said. "I'm sorry you lost your nice brooch."

"It served me right. George didn't want me to take it. One nice thing about my husband is that he never says 'I told you so'."

"Apart from the robbery, was the trip a success?"

"Yes and no. We started off by doing too much too fast. It wasn't until we met this man named Oliver Anvil that we learned how to sightsee the right way. When I say the right way, I mean the way cultured people go about it. They don't just follow the guide books. They do what George is doing now – a bit late. They read up the history, which includes knowing which kings reigned where and when, and for how long. This man Anvil knew it all. My head used to spin sometimes, but I took in all I was capable of taking in."

"You often see the name Anvil in Crane," Kathryn remarked.

"Yes. On shops and villas. He said he used to live here – he left when he was nine. His grandfather was the Anvil who owned a lot of property in the district. Actually we bought our land from him. I hope Oliver will pay us a visit – you'll like him." She turned towards the house. "Well, back to the job."

"Are these flowers enough?"

"Yes, thanks. Let me take them inside and put them into vases."

"Why don't you stay out here for a little while? It's such a nice day."

"I've got to go in – Maureen Bolt's coming to do my hair. I wish I had hair like yours, that doesn't need hairdressers." She paused on her way indoors. "Before you go to lunch, come in and tell me if you like the new colour I'm painting the hall."

Kathryn said she would, and set about weeding a flower-bed. After a time she looked up to see Christopher Hobart standing beside her.

She frowned. This made the fourth consecutive day. She had done her best to indicate that she did not want company when she was working, but she was beginning to think he was too dense to take hints. Either that, or he was deliberately ignoring them.

"Good morning," he said.

"Good morning."

"Nice day."

"If you say so."

"Can't you see? Sunshine and blue sky. It must be nice to work in a garden in this weather."

"Weather," she told him, "makes very little difference to

professional gardeners. They have to work, weather or no weather. If you want to see Stella, she's in the house."

"Well actually, I came to see you."

She rose from her knees and looked up at him. He was a tall man, so there was a long way to look. She noticed for the first time that there was a tinge of auburn in his hair. She also noted that his eyes were grey, his nose was rather long, and his ears stuck out. No Adonis.

"What did you want to see me about?" she enquired coldly.

"Well . . . this and that. It occurred to me while I was shaving that you can't interrupt a man who's counting up a row of figures, but you can talk to a girl who's pulling up weeds."

"Who's looking after your bookshop?"

"My assistant. I have to have a break now and then."

She thought of asking him to take it elsewhere, but something in his manner – a combination of confidence, hope and shyness – stopped her.

"I suppose," he said, "you couldn't have lunch with me one day? Or dinner?"

"One day. Perhaps. How long do you take for your break?"

"Break? Oh, not long. Am I in your way?"

"I don't want you to neglect your bookshop."

"If you don't want me hanging about," he told her calmly, "you've only got to say so. But you're not an easy girl to . . . to get to know. If you want the truth, I've been trying for some time to work up enough courage to ask you to come out with me, but it's only recently that I believe you aren't quite so busy at weekends." He paused deliberately for a moment so that she would realise he was referring to Aubrey Roach before continuing, "Anyway, I thought that might mean you may have time for someone like me."

There was a somewhat chilly silence. "Perhaps you could think it over," he suggested anxiously.

63

"All right."

She walked away, only to find that he was following her. She sat on the wall which Stella had been sitting on and gave an exasperated sigh. What she needed, she thought, was a fly swat.

He seated himself beside her. Then he spoke in a conversational tone.

"What made you decide to be a gardener?" he enquired.

She gave up; he was clearly determined to stay, even if she wouldn't agree to go out with him.

"Chance," she answered. "I suppose you heard that my mother wanted to start a boutique here, but old Mrs. Russell had got in first and didn't want any competition."

"Old battle-axe, Mrs. Russell."

"Well, she won the battle against my mother. Instead of going back to London, as my mother did, I asked George to give me a job as a gardener. So here I am." There was another silence. Then: "What made you become the owner of a bookshop?" she asked.

"I was half-owner of a bookshop in Cambridge. The other half decided to go back to his native Scotland, and I sold everything I had and bought him out. I was strongly advised not to come to a backwater like Outercrane, but there was too much competition in Cambridge and – or so it seemed to me – not nearly so much here. So I sold the Cambridge shop and to my surprise made a fat profit – and here I am, like you. The second-hand department I opened paid off. I knew it would. You should come and count the number of people who spend time browsing among the books. On a sunny day like this, I put out a table with second-hand books on them, and it looks like a scene from a Paris print." He paused. "I liked the way you reacted when I dropped a dozen heavy books on your head. 'That', I said to myself, 'is a girl I'd like to know more about.' So here I am, getting to know about you."

She turned to study him.

64

"What happens if I don't want to know you?" she asked.

"Nothing. I'd fade into the distance. But I'm banking on the fact that I'm not an unlikeable kind of fellow. I pay my debts, I say my prayers, I give alms to the poor and I've never been had up for assault. *And* most important of all, I'm making a success of my bookshop." He looked at the expanse of garden round them. "You can't possibly manage all this on your own."

"Of course I can't. It's nearly five acres. But a lot of it, as you can see, is half wild – that wooded part that George decided to leave as it was. It's more than an acre – it connects with a path from the back of Willie Bolt's shop, and drops down to the road that runs beside the church. Apart from that acre, there's the walled garden and there's the vegetable garden. I can manage those. Ken does the lawn-mowing. He also does the digging in his spare time."

"He'll have more spare time from now on. He's been sacked from that restaurant."

"I know. When George heard that, he took him on full-time until October."

"That's good news. Is Ken here now?"

"Yes. What made you decide to go and live in his grandmother's house? Everyone knows she's an appalling cook."

"Her cooking doesn't worry me. She keeps the house clean and all I ask her to provide are snack meals. If I want anything more, I go out and get it. I refurnished the rooms I live in, and made them comfortable. How did the Deepleys' trip to Naples go?"

She hesitated.

"I don't think it was much of a success," she said at last. "Stella didn't tell me much about it, but even before the robbery – you know she lost a valuable brooch?"

"Yes."

"Even before that, I think that things weren't what they'd hoped. They found themselves pretty much on their own until they ran into someone who knew Crane and had once lived there."

"I heard someone say something about him in the shop. He was one of the Anvils, wasn't he?"

"Yes."

"The old grandfather was very rich, but I don't think he left his money to his family. I heard it all went to zoological societies."

She rose.

"I'm going back to work."

He left her reluctantly. Going back to weeding, she realised with a feeling of surprise that she was sorry to see him go. But with the surprise was mingled anger against herself for having allowed him to make an impression, however slight, on her. She was just beginning to recover from her regret at having spent so much time with Aubrey Roach. She had been a fool to imagine that she could keep their relationship on a purely friendly basis. He had become troublesome, and it was hard to shake him off now – but the fault was not his; it was hers. She had never for a moment imagined herself in love with him – she had merely drifted into the habit of seeing him whenever he appeared in the town. She did not want, now, to become involved with any other man. Christopher Hobart might be as hard as Aubrey to shake off, but she must find some way of keeping him out of the garden.

Her musings were interrupted by the appearance at the gate of Maureen Bolt, who had come to wash and set Stella's hair.

"Hi!" she called out to Kathryn in her pleasant, husky voice. "How's things?"

Maureen was eighteen, a plump, plain girl who admitted her lack of looks but claimed cheerfully that she made the most of what she had. This she attempted to achieve by copying the clothes of the current fashion models, so that what Kathryn saw, watching her as she made her way to the house, were skin-tight green trousers, a blue and white striped sweater, scarlet and white canvas shoes and hair tortured into a style that resembled tangled barbed wire.

"Where's your car?" Kathryn called to her.

"Sick. My sister drove me here in our van, and she's going to pick me up at Mrs. Woodley's, my next stop."

Maureen had worked for a time with her sister in their father's shop. Tiring of this, she had ignored her father's protests and threats and gone to London to stay with an aunt who ran a hairdressing salon. Here she took a crash course in hairdressing. Returning home, she bought a small car and, like Mrs. Truedom, set herself up in business, making an arrangement with a local hairdresser to go to the homes of clients who preferred home treatment rather than going to the salon. However, she treated her customers with scant respect; she feared nobody, not even her formidable father. Her one weakness seemed to be her long-standing relationship with Kenneth Preston. The two had maintained a curious stop-go affair for more than three years.

"Where's Ken?" she asked Kathryn, joining her by the flower-bed.

"Inside the house."

"I suppose you've heard the bad news?"

"Yes, but –"

"He's got a coconut where his head ought to be, that's what's the matter with him. He was warned about getting chummy with the customers, but would he listen? Not him. Wait till I see him – I'll tell him a thing or two."

"How did you know he –"

"– got the push? He phoned me at the shop before I left this morning, and told me. He was afraid to tell me to my face."

"Before you get too cross with him, I should tell you that Mr. Deepley has given him a full-time job here until October."

"Mr. Deepley has?"

"Yes."

"Then he'll be working under you?"

"I suppose so."

"Well, that ought to be a job he can stick to. He likes being outside. But if it lasts till October, I'll eat my hat — only I haven't got one. Here he comes. Look at him — grinning all over his face as though the restaurant had made a partner out of him. Hi, you," she continued as Ken reached them, "d'you know what you are? You're what they call one of life's failures. You're a throw-out in the dustbin of life. You're —"

He put his arms round her. She attempted to fend him off with the large canvas bag she carried on her rounds, but he evaded it, and gave her a hearty kiss.

"What I am," he told her, "is under-gardener to Mr. Deepley, Esquire."

"Lemme go. I'm finished with you." She freed herself and looked up at him angrily. "Years ago, when my dad heard I was letting you come after me, he called you a perambulating parasite and told you to 'op off and get yourself a job somewhere else — if you could. I stuck up for you, but I was a fat fool to do it. Let's face it: you're a wash-out."

"That's right," Ken said encouragingly. "Get it off your chest and then we can get the train back on the line."

"You can get the train back yourself. I'm through."

Ken addressed Kathryn.

"She loves me," he explained. "This is just her way of showing it. Here," he caught Maureen's arm as she began to walk away, "where're you off to?"

"To do Mrs. Deepley's hair — where else? I'm a hair-dresser, remember? Lemme go. I'm late."

He released her.

"I'll still be here when you come out," he told her. "Try not to be too long." He turned to Kathryn. "At your

68

service," he announced. "Just tell me what you want done."

Maureen went into the house and made her way to Stella's bedroom.

"Mornin', love," she said breezily. "Everything all right with you and Mr. Deepley?"

"Yes, thank you, Maureen."

"I've brought a new shampoo I want to try out on you. Let's start washing you, shall we?"

In the bathroom, applying the shampoo vigorously as Stella bent under the shower, she told her what she thought of Ken.

"I know he's no good," she said, "but if you're stuck on a guy, well, you are and that's it, whether he's in a job or on the dole. Sometimes I think I'm only going with him to spite my dad. Nice smell this has got, hasn't it?"

"Uh-hu."

This was usually all the contribution Stella made to the weekly conversation. If she had wanted to talk, it would have been difficult, for Maureen, once in her stride, was difficult to stop.

"Nice hair you've got. Not like some of the ladies I do. Just thatch or straw, some of 'em." She applied hair conditioner. "I wish you'd let me do it the way I want to. You'd look real fashionable. Trouble in a place like this is that there's nobody who as you might say gives a lead that the other ladies can follow. They keep to the same old styles, year after year – I wonder they don't get sick of 'em. It doesn't – can you put your head forward a bit? That's better – it doesn't gimme a chance to show what I can do if I'm let. That too hot for you? As I said, I could try out new styles. Anyone can do what I do all the time – just wash and same old set. It's not as if I just picked up hairdressing, like all the girls in the salons here. I had a proper training. But I'll never get a chance to use it."

She wrapped Stella's hair in a towel and led her to the dressing table in the bedroom.

69

"It smells nice," Stella remarked.

"It's a good make. You have to pay more, but it's well worth it. Sure you wouldn't like me to take it up at the sides – like this – and give you some little curls on top?"

"No, thank you."

"Pity. You're so pretty, you could carry it, like. But if you won't, you won't. I haven't said thank you to you and Mr. Deepley for giving Ken a job in the garden."

"We're glad to have him."

"That's what everyone says when they take him on. Mind you, he'll be all right in a garden. He's good at digging and hoeing and what not. He doesn't know much about growing flowers, but he gets some good vegetables out of his grandmum's patch. She never thanks him – all she does is grumble because he didn't sow more. My dad calls her a garrulous grouser. Hope he knows what it means. I dunno where he gets all those big words he uses."

"Is he still trying to keep you away from Ken?"

"Fat chance. That's one reason I left the shop and took up this job – so's I could meet Ken any time, any place. I don't tell my dad that. He must know, I dare say, but he's afraid to go too far when he's talking about him. He's frightened I'd leave him altogether."

"I can sympathise with him in a way. Ken isn't what most people would regard as a marriageable proposition. I'm very fond of him, but –"

"Yeah, that's it. *But*. Well, he got under my skin, I dunno how, and I can't get him out. I've tried going out with two or three other fellows in this town, but I never found one I could get on with the way I get on with Ken, even if we do fight most of the time. I suppose you could say I'm in love. Close your eyes a minute – I'm going to give you just a touch of hair spray. There you are. That's the lot."

She took the money Stella gave her, put it into her purse and went towards the door.

70

"Can I go out the back door?" she asked. "Ken's out front, waiting for me. It won't do him no harm to wait for nothing. Maybe he'll do some work for a change. Bye, love. See you same time next week."

5

Three days later, Stella returned from an expedition to the town and sought out George. She found him in the garden planting out sweetpea seedlings. As she reached him, the low clouds that had been threatening rain all the morning broke, and a sharp shower descended.

"Inside," ordered George. "I'll finish this job when summer returns."

They hurried into the house.

"Coffee in the kitchen," said Stella.

This was always a sign that she wanted to tell him something she considered important. He followed her in silence.

"George," she said when they were seated, "I've had the most wonderful idea."

"Good. What is it?"

"I was coming out of the butcher's when I ran into Mrs. Woodley. We stopped to talk."

"And she gave you the wonderful idea?"

"No. While we were talking, I just happened to notice that she was wearing a piece of enamel jewellery – a very plain pattern, but beautifully coloured. And suddenly I thought of Aunt Mary."

"God rest her soul," said George piously. "I wonder if she knows her naval brooch was swiped?"

"Don't change the subject."

"I thought Aunt Mary was the subject."

"Not her. Enamel jewellery. Don't you remember that she had several pieces?"

"Pieces of what?"

"Enamel jewellery. Look, if you're not interested, I'll stop."

72

"Don't stop. Proceed. Aunt Mary had several pieces. So?"

"She not only wore them – she *made* them. I'd completely forgotten it was a hobby of hers. She tried to interest me in it, but at that time I was too busy to listen. But today, looking at Mrs. Woodley's, I thought: Why don't I?"

"Why don't you what?"

"Make them. It's *fascinating*. Diana Woodley said she used to make them too, and she offered to show me what I'd have to do."

"And having made them, are you going to deck yourself in enamel jewellery?"

"No, silly. I'm going to learn how to do it, and then I'm going to sell what I make for charity. I should make a lot of money – and I'd have something interesting to do, and it would bring in something that I can donate."

"I see. When do you begin?"

She studied him.

"You're not taking this seriously, are you?" she enquired.

"Not very. It doesn't sound like you – enamel jewellery."

"Well, I can't wait to learn. Diana Woodley said she'd come and teach me – or at any rate, start me off."

Mrs. Woodley was not long in appearing. She came two days later, as well-dressed and well-groomed as usual, entered the house after a perfunctory knock and tracked George and Stella to the library.

"Here I am," she announced. "I've been reading up my old notebooks, and I was surprised to find how much I remembered. But I've jotted down a few items, just in case."

Groping in her capacious handbag, she produced several sheets of paper.

"It's a good idea for Stella to lose herself in something really interesting, isn't it?" she asked George.

"A very good idea."

"She couldn't have hit on a better person to help her.

Look —" she bent forward to exhibit to George the necklace she was wearing — "this is the last thing I made. I would have gone on, but I made the mistake of marrying, and for the next year or so I was sailing round the world with my husband. Incidentally, I have to report that he's on his way home."

"Oh, is he? Good," said George. He liked Clive Woodley.

"It isn't *good* at all," Mrs. Woodley snapped. "Sometimes I think he's psychic — he chooses the worst possible times to put in an appearance, and he expects me to drop everything I'm doing and give over my entire life to him."

"When is he coming?" George asked.

"He's arriving this morning on the eleven fifty-five. He cabled asking me to meet him. Wouldn't you have thought that after navigating half-way round the Caribbean, he'd be able to find his own way from the station to his house? So I haven't much time, Stella. Tell me, where do you propose working?"

"I hadn't thought of —"

"I began by thinking that all I'd need would be a large table. I found that was nonsense. You'll want to give it two tables at least, which means that you'll need a work-room. How about one of those rooms on the top floor? They're all empty now, aren't they?"

"Yes."

"Could you use one as a work-room?"

"I don't see why not."

"Splendid. Let's go up."

Stella led the way. Mrs. Woodley followed, and George found himself sucked into the stream. They stopped at the first guest room, a pleasant and sunny apartment with windows overlooking the drive.

"Perfect. Couldn't be better," pronounced Mrs. Woodley. She turned to Stella. "To begin with," she told her, "you'll have to write down the equipment you'll need. Have you a paper and pen?"

George produced them.

"First, of course," went on Mrs. Woodley, "you'll need a kiln."

"*Kiln?*" George echoed. "Did you say a kiln?"

"That's right. A kiln. You can buy a small one that's adequate for our purpose. There are, of course, more elaborate ones, but they cost more and they use more electricity. Kiln. Got that down?"

"Yes," said Stella.

"I must say I enjoyed making jewellery, when I was doing it. I'm sorry I gave it up. Speaking of giving up, isn't it time somebody told Ruth Russell that she ought to give up driving? She practically ran into my car when I was on my way here – she was swerving about in the middle of the road as usual. She's a public menace when she's at the wheel of that juggernaut of hers. Where was I? Oh, the kiln. What I advise you to get is an electric kiln with a metal hood. You can buy all the separate parts – not in Crane, but in a shop I'll take you to in London. Heating coil, surface, hood. Write those down. Ready?"

"Yes."

Mrs. Woodley consulted her notes.

"Now where are we? Yes, here. We could have gone up to London today if my husband hadn't chosen this particular day to come back. Last time, it was when I'd invited two friends of mine to stay. I had to put them off – he would have gone out of his way to be unpleasant. Not that he'd have to go far. I wouldn't say this to anyone but you two, but you know already that he doesn't exactly spread sunshine when he's around. I think sometimes a divorce would make things easier, but I couldn't live comfortably on the alimony he could give me – besides which, I always feel sorry for women left without men to provide the odd escort. Now let me see," she went on, consulting her notes. "Next, Stella, you'll need a feeding rod."

"What's a feeding rod?" Stella enquired.

75

"You use it to lift the metal hood off the kiln when the firing's done. You'll also need a firing tray – that's to use for the small pieces. And tongs – am I going too fast for you?"

"No. What will I use tongs for?"

"They're for holding the pieces during the tempering process. Next, a slide for putting the enamel pieces on the kiln and taking them off again. Next, an asbestos pad to put the pieces on to cool." She paused for breath. "Now we come to cutting the shapes. I advise you keep them simple. It's no use doing as I did, starting off with elaborate designs; keep them *simple*." She glanced at her wrist-watch. "My God, is that the time? I'll have to hurry. I do think it's hard, the way he disappears for months at a time and then comes back and disrupts my life. I was a fool to marry him. Heaven knows I had plenty of other men after me. As I said, Stella, keep the designs simple. Get two pairs of metal shears, curved and straight – all right?"

"Yes."

"And you'll need pliers, round-nosed and flat-nosed."

"Is that all?" George enquired, with a touch of incredulous sarcasm.

"No. Write down metal file, calipers, an awl and a wooden mallet."

"It sounds," George ventured, "an awful lot of equipment for merely making –"

"Do keep out of this, George," Mrs. Woodley snapped irritably. "Did you think Stella would be able to work without tools?"

"No, but –"

"Then for God's sake let's get on. A sieve, Stella – that's for the enamel powder. You'll also need metal adhesive. And tragacanth."

"Traga . . .?"

"Otherwise known as gum," George told her. "Tragacanth," he went on in a sermonising voice, "is the name

76

given to the mucilaginous or gummy substance derived from certain shrubs found in western Asia."

"Very knowledgeable, I'm sure," said Mrs. Woodley coldly. "You must have been brought up by my husband's methods: 'If you want to interest a boy in anything scientific, give him a bucket of sea water and a powerful microscope and that'll start him off.' Could we briefly discuss metals, Stella? The best materials are sheet copper or sterling silver. *Not* brass. Brass is unsuitable, I've forgotten why."

George spoke again.

"Because its melting point is –"

"Yes, yes, yes." Mrs. Woodley spoke impatiently. "You can tell Stella later. Now we come to the enamel. There are several kinds. There's the opaque and the transparent and the opalescent. I can explain about these when I start you off on the work. Your first job will be preparing the metal, but before we get to that, you and I, Stella, must take a trip up to London and buy all those things on your list." She took a much-needed deep breath. "And that's all I've got time to tell you now. As soon as I get rid of Clive, I'll ring you and we'll fix a day for going up to this shop I know. Now I'll be off, and on the way to the station I'll compose my face into a welcoming beam, to impress any of the local population who happen to be standing round. Goodbye."

"Goodbye – and thank you," said Stella.

They accompanied her to the front door and watched her get into her car.

"Tall order," George remarked, his eyes on the papers in Stella's hand.

She was watching the car out of sight.

"Odd sort of marriage, isn't it?" she remarked.

"It seems to suit them both. He comes home to golf and squash and then takes off for some more sea air, and she's left to live the way she wants to live. Are you still hankering to make enamel jewellery?"

"More than ever. If you like, you can sit down and draw me some simple designs that I can start on."

As it happened, Clive Woodley's stay was briefer than usual. The journey to the London shop was soon accomplished. Stella then set up her work tables. Mrs. Woodley was in attendance in the early stages, but left after a time to visit friends in Scotland.

"Remember, don't go too fast," she enjoined Stella before leaving. "You're showing great promise – but you're a bit too ambitious. As I told you, keep it simple. See you when I get back."

George, to his surprise, found himself interested in the project. His first intention in going up to watch Stella at work had been to give her encouragement, but he discovered that she was too intent on what she was doing to notice whether he was there or not. He made his way to the garden and took Kathryn into his confidence.

"Wonderful," he said, "to see her giving her mind to something new. Do you need any enamel bracelets, necklaces, rings?"

"The truth," she said, "is that I'm not too keen on enamel jewellery."

"You surprise me. I would have said the colours would appeal to you. Myself, I like the exotic look of the finished pieces. Kind of Mexican or Red Indian."

"Stella said the equipment was expensive."

"She understated. I thought at first that Mrs. Woodley was making it all up, but I see that Stella's using everything she bought."

"Why does her husband come and go?"

"More accurately, he goes and comes. He came here when he retired from the Navy, and he appeared to settle – but it seems that what he saw round him didn't please him. He decided that our life style – in fact, the life style of a great part of the western world – was too artificial. This business of commuting and playing rounds of golf and meeting for evening drinks and so on was, he decided, a frail structure – am I telling this well?"

"Yes. Go on."

"A frail structure which would collapse at the first serious challenge."

"A nuclear bomb?"

"No. He thought, thinks, that another war would do it. He said, says, that we're all cushioned, all looking out for more and more comforts, instead of pitting ourselves against the elements."

"As he does?"

"As he does. When you think of it, it must be disconcerting, to say the least, to complete a voyage round, say, the Horn and come back to find the milk and the bread delivered on the doorstep."

"I suppose it is."

"And then there's something else that plagues him: the attitude most people have towards alms-giving. In a word, charity. He says we dole out a small portion of our bonus, instead of carving a piece out of our living standards, and sharing it."

"The Harleys would agree with that."

"I dare say. But Clive Woodley's no evangelist. What he thinks, he thinks, but only his closest friends hear about it. He sticks it for as long as he can, and then he has to go off and resume his battle with the elements. Everyone's rather relieved when he's gone – his wife most of all – but he's here long enough to disturb our consciences, if we've got any. If he had a different temperament, I dare say he'd get up on a soap box and preach – and in my view, it wouldn't be a bad thing. But instead of that, he slopes off, back to his ocean-going yacht, leaving us all wondering how much we should put into the collection box at church next Sunday."

"I don't suppose he's the only one with misgivings about the way we live. My father was glad that he'd lived – he said – to see the working man become the boss."

"So am I – but all the working man seems to me to be doing is making things better for himself. From penury to comfort to luxury, from luxury to decadence, from decadence to –"

"– to the collapse of the frail structure?"

"Exactly. How did we get on to this?"

"The Woodleys. And before them, enamel necklaces."

"That's right. Stella's new interest."

"Do you think she'll keep it up?"

George nodded.

"Yes, I do. She's already talking about giving a sort of exhibition and selling the pieces she's made. Thank God she's found something to interest her."

Stella was soon to find another outlet for her energy.

"George," she said, a few evenings later, "I've been thinking over something you said – that I might consider taking up painting again. Working on this jewellery has turned my mind to colours."

They were in his study. He closed the cheque book he had been using, put it into a pigeon hole in his desk, and gave her his attention.

"Funny you should mention painting," he told her. "I dropped into the bookshop this morning and found Christopher talking to an odd-looking chap. He introduced me to him. It appears he's a Russian who came over a couple of years ago on a cargo ship and skipped ashore at Southampton – and never went back. He's been living in Crane ever since. His papers appear to be in order and he's been scratching a living doing translations. He's got a room in a sort of boarding house somewhere out of town."

"What's that got to do with my taking up painting again?"

"His pre-refugee profession was painting. He started off here by trying to get pupils, but there was no response. Christopher said he was a top-class painter, so why not meet him and sound him out?"

"What, ask him to give me lessons?"

"Not exactly. If he's as good as Christopher says he is, you could explain that you're thinking of taking up painting again as a hobby after many years, and would like a bit of guidance. If he's short of money – and he looks as though he is – he's not likely to refuse."

She took a few moments to think it over.

"I might," she said.

When next she saw Christopher, she brought up the subject of the Russian.

"George told you about him?" Christopher asked.

"He told me all he knew, or all you knew, which wasn't much."

"His name's Rostov, but he calls himself Ross. His written English is perfect, and at the moment he's doing translations – but he talks the language so badly that you can hardly make out what he's saying. That was one thing, I think, that wrecked his idea of getting pupils for painting. The other disqualifying factor was his appearance – he's very tall and broad but at the same time, he's painfully thin and his clothes hang on him, and he's got a very forbidding expression. Ferocious, in fact. I got the definite impression that he hadn't been eating properly. But if you want to get in touch with him, I'll arrange a meeting."

No meeting was arranged, but with Mr. Ross's address, given to her by Christopher, Stella drove through Crane to a small village set in the middle of a heath. It was not a picturesque place; apparently there were plans to develop it, for piles of bricks were stacked on various sites, and one or two old houses had scaffolding round them. At the end of a line of small shops was one which was called "The Bakery". On the upper storey Stella could just make out the sign: *Boarders*. This must be it.

She stopped the car, stepped round the piles of rubble at one side of the baker's entrance, and found a flight of wooden stairs leading to the upper part of the building. At the top was a door with most of its paint peeling off, and a knocker in the form of a sea lion. In response to her summons, the door was opened by a slovenly woman in a soiled floral overall.

"Yes?" she enquired, her tone belligerent.

"Good morning. Does Mr. Ross live here?"

"D'you want to see 'im?"

"Yes please. Is he in?"

"'e's always in. 'e does 'is work 'ere." The door opened more widely. "Come this way."

Stella followed her along a narrow and malodorous passage, to a door at the end. The woman gave a brief knock, opened the door, said "Someone to see you", ushered Stella in and banged the door behind her. Stella stood there in stunned silence.

The room faced north and was so dark that an electric light bulb hanging from the ceiling was necessary to provide illumination enough for reading. The furnishings were scanty, and drab. A narrow bed stood against one wall, one end of it against the side of a cupboard whose door was wedged with a piece of cardboard. A washstand occupied the space below the grimy window. In the middle of the room was a large table covered with neatly stacked papers. At this sat a man, lank and extremely thin, wearing the frowning look that Christopher had described. After blinking at Stella in bewilderment for some moments, he pushed back his chair and rose to his feet.

"Good morning. I'm sorry to disturb you," Stella began. "My name is Stella Deepley. I would have phoned to say I was coming, but Mr. Hobart said there was no telephone here."

His emaciated appearance had roused all her motherly instincts. She longed to set him down in front of a good, hot, nourishing meal.

"Telephone?" Mr. Ross, standing by the table and appearing to be holding on to it for support, shook his head. "No. No telephone. Please to sit."

There was only one chair in the room – the one on which he had been sitting. He pushed it forward and then stood waiting for her to state her business.

"You wish translations?" he enquired.

"No."

"This is all I do – translations. Perhaps you have come to the wrong place. You have mistaken."

Stella, without appearing to look, was taking in details that horrified her. There was no carpet or rug on the floor. The towel hanging by the washstand was little more than a rag. There were damp patches on the walls. Mr. Ross was wearing carpet slippers – one pair of shoes could be seen under the bed.

"I came," she said slowly, "because Mr. Hobart said . . ."

"Mr. –?"

"Hobart. He owns the bookshop."

"Ah. Ho-bart. He said?"

"He told me that you were once a painter. I used to paint – not very well – when I was young, and I'm thinking of taking it up again. My children are all married and living at the other end of the world, and I've got a lot of time on my hands. I wondered whether it would be possible, if I decided to try and paint again, for you to give me a few lessons?" She gave a glance round the room. "It would mean coming to my house – I live in Crane – but if you have no transport, I'd come and fetch you and bring you back again."

She stopped. There was a long silence. Mr. Ross was staring at her, but appeared unable to find anything to say.

"Perhaps," she suggested, "your translations keep you too busy to allow you to –"

"I am not too busy."

"Then –?"

"But I do not understand." As Christopher had told her, his English was mangled, but she could follow what he was saying. "I do not understand. You wish to paint?"

83

"Yes." If she hadn't been sure before coming to this appallingly dreary room, she told herself, she was sure now. "Yes, I do."

"But . . . are you saying that you need a teacher for this painting?"

"What I want," she said, "is someone – someone like yourself, who is or has been a good painter – to come now and then to see what I'm doing, and tell me if I'm doing anything wrong. There are no art teachers in the district. I –"

"No. There are none. But they want none. I myself tried, at first, to have . . . what is the word? Pupils. But there was nobody. Nobody."

"That's what I thought – until Mr. Hobart told me about you. I hope you won't refuse to help me."

"No. That I will not do – refuse. To paint – once that was my whole life. Now there is only the translations, to bring money."

"We haven't mentioned fees," Stella said, "but –"

"Please?"

"Fees. It would be impossible to ask you to undertake this, Mr. Ross, unless you charged me fees for the lessons."

"Fees. You are speaking of payment?"

"Yes. I've no idea what you would charge, but I could find out what the proper fees are, and then we could discuss the matter. But you haven't told me whether you can help me or not."

"Help you? This I do not know. I do not know what help you will need. I do not know what skill you have, or if you have none at all."

"I'm not bad – but I'd like to be better. Have you a free day once a week?"

"Yes. If I had not, I would make one, because you have spoken of payment, which will help me to live better. You have spoken of coming to take me to your house, and to bring me back. Without this, there would be only the public omnibus which goes only very early in the morning and comes back only late at night. My translation work – this goes by the post."

Stella stood up.

"Then all that's left," she said, "is to fix the day of the week."

"You may say any one of the days."

"Would every Wednesday suit you?"

"It is for you to be suited – not me. Yes, Wednesday."

"I'll come for you at eleven thirty. We could get in some work before lunch – I hope you'll have lunch with me – and we could work afterwards. I'll bring you back here at three o'clock."

Back home to tea, she thought miserably, drunk from the cracked mug she could see among his papers on the table.

The Russian saw Stella to the door and watched as she went down the flight of steps. She drove away, taking with her the picture of the ill-dressed figure, the comfortless room, the seedy house and the grim little village.

She gave a somewhat impassioned account of the visit to George. After calming her down, he went to see Christopher.

"It's your fault," he told him. "You sent her there, knowing –"

"I'd never seen the place. I only knew him because he sometimes comes to the shop."

"You knew he was a waif of some kind. One only has to look at him to guess that. So off she went, and of course it was a dump and she came back in a state."

"A state of what?"

"Well, several states. Pity. Fury because the poor man has to live in such discomfort. Disgust because his landlady looked a slattern and not a nice, homely, cheerful woman who'd mother him. Now we're stuck with him every Wednesday, lunch included. You wait and see: Stella will feed him on caviare and steak – and she's paying him, or proposing to pay him, four times what I reckon he's worth."

"If it means that she's taking up painting again, won't it be worth it?"

"*If.* She's not thinking about her own painting at the moment. She's turned the furniture out of one of the top floor rooms next to her work-room and made a studio out of it. Now she's going round trying to whip up more pupils. All this, mark you, before she even knows whether he can paint and whether he can teach."

"I wouldn't know about the teaching part of it. But I once saw some of his work – he sold two paintings through me – and I can guarantee that he's good. More than good."

Stella, after concluding her arrangements for the reception of Mr. Ross, held a belated consultation with George.

"You won't mind having him here once a week, will you?"

"Thank you for asking. No, I won't mind. What made you ask – at last?"

"Well, I remembered that you said you liked having the house to ourselves."

"So I do. But what's a Russian every Wednesday?"

"But there's something else, George."

"Not another Russian?"

"No. But while I was fixing the room, I remembered that when I was talking to Miss Minter at the wedding, she told me she paints."

"I know she paints. Didn't you see all her efforts on the walls of their house when they sold it? Awful stuff it was, too. You're not thinking of enlisting her as a pupil for this Russian, are you?"

"Why not? She loves painting, but there's no room in that little place where they're living to spread herself out with easel and canvases and so on. Couldn't I tell her that for, say, one day a week there's an empty studio here where she can bring her equipment and work?"

"With a teacher to guide her?"

86

"No. At least, I hadn't thought of it from the teacher angle. But would you mind if I suggested it to her?"

"Why should I mind? She'll hardly be in my way, up there, will she?"

"No. I'd make it clear to her that she could come and go as she pleased. I'd let her in when she came and she could let herself out."

"You do as you please – as long as you're happy."

"Don't you think it's a good idea?"

"Let's call it a kind thought. Can she leave her mother alone while she puts in hours painting?"

"Yes. Her mother's fully occupied making – and selling – dolls' clothes."

"Will you give Miss Minter lunch, like your Russian?"

"No."

"Then I'll go as far as saying it's a good idea."

Miss Minter, when told of the offer, thought it a splendid idea, and put forward a suggestion of her own.

"Why," she enquired timidly, "can't I enrol myself for lessons? I would so love to find someone who would help me improve my work. I realise how far short it falls of even a beginner's standard. Couldn't I arrange an occasional lesson with this Russian gentleman?"

Stella hesitated. The fees she had decided on were more than Mr. Ross was likely to earn elsewhere. Miss Minter read her thoughts.

"If you're worried I can't afford to pay for the lessons, I assure you that I shall be able to meet them without difficulty. Please believe me. I'll make economies which will enable me to do something I shall enjoy more than anything in the world."

"One more pupil," George reported to Christopher. "What's the betting she doesn't stop at one?"

So Mr. Ross found himself on the following Wednesday morning with two pupils instead of one. Conducted by Stella up to the studio, he set up his easel, placed a half-finished picture on it and, for the first time since his arrival, spoke.

"We are ready," he announced. "We shall begin."

He began by examining the small oil painting that Miss Minter had put on her easel. His expression, always forbidding, became positively menacing.

"No good," he pronounced. "You have more canvas?"

"M-more canvas? Oh yes, yes."

In a few strokes, he demonstrated what he wished her to do. Then he turned to the half dozen of Stella's pictures stacked against the wall. From these he selected one, placed it on the easel and indicated where improvements could be made.

They worked for the most part in silence. Shortly before one o'clock, Stella slipped away to complete the preparations she had made for lunch. Miss Minter, who had not accepted Stella's invitation to stay, was driven home by George, who then returned to join his wife and Mr. Ross in the dining room.

At half past three, Stella drove away with her painting master and on her return, reported on the morning's progress.

"He's good," she told George. "He scarcely utters a word, but he shows you exactly what you're doing wrong."

"What did he make of Miss Minter?"

"Mincemeat. But she's tougher than she looks. She realised that she'd have to start from scratch, and she did everything he told her to do. She's determined to improve."

These peaceful meetings went on undisturbed for some time – and then two more pupils were added to the group. Mr. and Mrs. Harley called one morning to see Stella.

"Sorry to hold you up if you're busy," Mr. Harley apologised. "We won't keep you long. The fact is that we dropped in to see old Mrs. Minter the other day, and saw some work – a couple of paintings – her daughter'd been doing under this Russian you got hold of to give you lessons. We talked it over, my wife and I, and we wondered if by any chance we could –"

"We'd like to get in touch with him," Mrs. Harley broke in. "We both paint a bit, and when the children go off to school, we find ourselves with plenty of time to –"

"– to indulge our hobby," finished Mr. Harley. "I understand Miss Minter works here – in your studio upstairs. Is there any chance of our coming in and joining the class?"

"It's hardly a class," Stella said. "At the moment, it's just Miss Minter and myself."

"Why?" Mr. Harley enquired. "Hobart – the bookshop Hobart – told me that this Russian is pretty badly off. Fees from two more pupils would be a help, wouldn't they?"

"We're serious about this," Mrs. Harley said. "I know Miss Minter came here because there wasn't room in her rabbit hutch of a house to spread her paints around. We've got room enough, but we want – we want –"

"We want a studio atmosphere," explained Mr. Harley. "We want a good teacher – which this fellow must be, if the improvement in Miss Minter's technique is anything to go by. We want regular hours – a kind of painting school. Would you – with George's agreement, of course – let us in?"

Stella hesitated. This was a new development, and she needed time to think it over. When the Harleys had gone, she went into the garden to seek out George.

"Why not?" was his response on hearing their proposition. "You like them and so does Miss Minter."

"If I agreed, I'd want to change the hours of the lessons."

"Which would mean depriving the teacher of that nourishing lunch you give him. But, if he's going to get more money in fees, he'll be able to buy his own lunch."

"I think I'll tell the Harleys they can come, but I'll try to keep the work schedule as it is now."

"Suit yourself. But the Harleys aren't people who'll do this for a time and then drop it. I think they'll stick."

"So do I. George –"

"Well?"

"I'd like to spread out a little. I'd like to take the last of those top rooms and –"

"– and rig it out as a second studio?"

"Yes."

"Then do it. My guess is that you'll need it."

"I don't need it at the moment. But I was thinking that there are other people like Miss Minter – people who would like to find space to paint. It isn't only the actual painting. It's –"

"I know. It's where they can keep their wet canvases and where they can store their half-done work. Go ahead – spread out if you want to."

"It means that more and more of the house –"

George put down the shears with which he had been working, and turned to face her.

"Forget about the house, love," he said. "It was built for a family and it housed them all happily for as long as they needed it – but they don't need it any more."

"But you wanted . . ."

"To keep it as our home – just the two of us. But it's too big for just the two of us. This idea of yours – a studio or studios – it's the best you've had. So stick to it. After the Harleys, there'll be others."

"You don't think the Harleys will pull out subscription lists, do you?"

"Not when they see Mr. Ross's threadbare suit. As I was saying, there'll be more people turning up to –"

"I don't want strangers. Only people we know. People who really need the space."

"Then provide it."

"And you won't mind?"

He gave one of his slow smiles.

"Have I," he asked her, "or have I not spent twenty-five years trying to make you understand that if you're happy, I'm happy?"

"Yes." She leaned over and dropped a kiss on his cheek. "I love you."

"Thank you. Now, with your permission, I'll get on with my work."

There was soon another applicant. Surprisingly, it was Mr. Vernon. After him, even more surprisingly, came Miss Grail. She telephoned one evening to ask if she might drop in to see Stella and George and have a talk.

She arrived at six thirty, and George poured drinks for all.

"I'm going to come straight to the point," she began. "I'm not getting any younger, and the time has come to make some changes in my life."

"It's happening to us all," George said.

"That's true. But I'm getting – in fact, I've got – beyond the point at which I can drive round the country to dog shows. So – with great regret – I'm giving up breeding my Afghan hounds. I'm closing my kennels. I shall still act as judge at shows whenever I'm asked, but my chief occupation from now on is going to be looking after my sister, who's coming to live with me, and indulging one or two hobbies I've had no time for during the past I-don't-care-to-count years. Painting is one of them." She turned to Stella – "I understand you've started an art club."

"Art club?" Stella shook her head. "All I've done is . . ."

"Well, whatever you call it, you've given studio room to a few people, and you've found a good teacher. I want to become a pupil. So will my sister, when she arrives next week. She's extremely good – which I admit I'm not. I would have approached this Russian – what does he call himself? –"

"Ross."

"– I would have gone straight to him and asked if he'd agree to give us lessons, but it would be far more agreeable to join this group you've got together." She picked up her glass and leaned back in her chair. "Is there any chance of our adding to the number? How many are you, by the way?"

"There's Miss Minter, Mr. Vernon, and the Harleys."

"And yourself – five. With my sister and myself, that would be seven. Do you think seven too many to use your rooms as studios?"

"No." It was George who answered the question. "In fact, I can't think of a better use for those unused rooms at the top of the house than turning them into studios or work-rooms. I think Stella has found a gap in the facilities of this town, and I'm all for her filling it on a permanent basis. My only interest in the project will be to see that she keeps the numbers down to a reasonable level. I'm convinced that more and more people will want to join what you've just christened an art club."

"We're not a particularly artistic community," Miss Grail said. "But I'm right when I say that a small art club is needed. If you'll forgive my saying so – after all, you haven't yet consented to have my sister and me – the hours are awkward for most people."

"I realise that," Stella said. "I could talk to Mr. Ross about changing them."

"I understand that he lunches with you. Perhaps you could begin by giving him lunch, and then the club members could come in the afternoon?"

"I'll talk to him," Stella said, nodding. "I don't think he'll raise any objection."

"Where does he live?" Miss Grail enquired.

"Out of town, in an awful little village about four miles away."

"And you provide transport?"

"Yes."

"Why does he have to live out of town?" Miss Grail asked. "I understand that – apart from giving lessons here – all he does is translations. Can't he find rooms in town where he can do them? For example, that woman who comes here once a week to work for you – doesn't she take lodgers? Mr. Hobart lives there, so it can't be too bad. Hasn't she got a room spare?"

Stella did not take long to answer. Her mind went back to the visit she had paid to the seedy quarters in which she had found the Russian, and in which he was still living.

"I'll ask her," she said. "I don't know whether she'll have a room she can let – there's only one spare one besides the ones that are rented by Christopher Hobart. There may be someone in it."

"If there is," Miss Grail said regally, "I'm sure they can be got out."

Instead of asking Mrs. Preston, Stella went to Christopher.

"The room's occupied," he told her. "But it won't be for long – the woman who's in it is going back to her home in Essex to look after an aged father – or it may be mother. But it's not much of a room. It's got a nice outlook onto the river – but the furniture and carpet have to be seen to be believed."

"Will she let me change them?"

"She let me do what I liked with my rooms when I rented them. I threw out most of the stuff that was there, used a paint roller on the walls and bought a carpet and some furniture."

"Will you ask her about the other room and let me know when it'll be free?"

The room's occupant departed two weeks later, and after an interview with Mrs. Preston, Stella moved in and – aided by Ken – did some redecorating. Only then did she approach Mr. Ross.

"You were very kind," she said, "about agreeing to

93

change your hours and to take on some extra pupils. But there's still a difficulty – you live so far away. I happened to hear of a room – in the same house as the one Mr. Hobart lives in – and it's not very expensive. Will you come with me and look at it?"

She took him to view the room. What his thoughts were as he stood at the door and surveyed the small round table, the office chair, the freshly painted walls, plain curtains and carpet and comfortable leather armchair could not be put on record, as he did not voice them. His only remark was:

"This I cannot pay for. It will be too expensive."

"You won't be paying Mrs. Preston," Stella told him. "When the room became free, Mr. Hobart made an arrangement with her – he took over all the rooms – the ones he lives in and this one – because he wanted to have the option of renting them himself to people he thought suitable."

"I am suitable?"

"Certainly. And I'm sure he won't overcharge you."

He moved in. The teaching hours at the newly-christened Crane art club were changed to Wednesday afternoons. The requests to join were, as George had prophesied, numerous, but he himself wrote the letters of refusal to unwanted applicants.

"The trick," he explained to Stella, "was in naming it a club and not a school. I'm doing the refusing because one of your weaknesses is that you can't refuse anybody anything. We – you – will keep the number down to twenty. If anybody drops out, you can fill the vacant place – but twenty is enough to keep it club-like, twenty is enough to fill the rooms, and enough to provide your Russian protégé with an adequate income. Do you agree?"

"No. Just a remark."

"Well?"

"I love you."

6

Early in his married life, George had realised that his wife would be spending a good deal of time in her kitchen. He had gone to some trouble and expense to make it a room picturesque enough to please her. He had put Dutch tiles round the walls, and had also installed a wood-burning stove in the half of the room that overlooked the drive, adding a built-in table, and benches covered in scarlet leather. At this table Mrs. Preston had eaten her daily lunch; at other times it had been a base for many conferences held between husband and wife.

However, he saw that if he wanted to find Stella now, he should no longer be looking in the kitchen. She could be found far more often in the room at the top of the house which had become known as her work-room. In fact, George frequently found himself making his way upstairs simply to watch what Stella was doing. On the work-room tables were spread the equipment she had bought under Mrs. Woodley's supervision. George had made some designs – the first, not easy enough for her purpose, had been abandoned in favour of the more simple drawings. He had watched with interest the process of tempering the copper sheeting with which Stella was to work, and had even helped to remove the black scale formed during the heating.

"There's more in it," he at last told her, "than meets the eye. What are you going to do next – a necklace?"

"No. That bracelet you designed."

He helped her cut the links from a sheet of copper, and rounded off the corners with a file. Then came the enamelling.

"You're getting better at this than I am!" she told him one morning.

"I know. So I'm expecting to be paid something before you write your cheque for the charities. Did you notice that I remembered to include the hinges in my calculations for the overall length?"

"Yes. Clever."

"Joining the links evenly is going to be tricky."

"I know. Do you like the colour I've chosen?"

"Yes. That's what I like about this job – it's full of strong colour. As I told Kathryn, Mexican or Red Injun. What do we do when we've finished the bracelet?"

"We?"

"That's what I said. Another bracelet?"

"No. A pendant."

"Good. That's a neat little kiln, isn't it?"

George did not intrude on the painting sessions, however. Listening at times from the work-room, he noted that Mr. Vernon, far from discoursing on politics, was working in silence. At rare intervals the voice of Mr. Ross could be heard. He did not, George noted, believe in using soft words to criticise the work of his pupils. Short, sharp and to the point, he was – but so far, nobody had thrown down their brushes and stalked out in a huff. The numbers had risen from seven to ten; the local doctor and his wife had joined the artists, and the addition of a talented local solicitor had raised the standard of the exhibits.

There was another matter of interest to the Deepley household. Every weekday, George noticed that whatever the weather, Christopher Hobart appeared in the garden. He did not stay long; he followed Kathryn as she worked, addressing remarks to her more often than not unresponsive back. The chap, George decided, was a real sticker. Her efforts to discourage him seemed to have no effect whatever.

Her efforts were not, Kathryn admitted to herself, strenuous. In fact, if he became discouraged and stayed away, she would miss him. But her resolve to allow an interval to pass before getting involved with any other man but Aubrey Roach had hardened. She had made a fool of herself once; she did not want to do so again.

In spite of this, she found that she had progressed from accepting Christopher's presence in the garden to inviting him to an occasional lunch in the gardener's cottage. She made sandwiches or a snack; they ate in the little living room on wet days, and on the bench outside when it was fine.

"Can I take it," he asked one morning, "that I no longer disturb you?"

"I'd probably work better if you stayed away. If you're so interested in gardening, why don't you give up book-selling and take it up? You'd find it a good deal harder than standing at a counter recommending the latest novels."

"Why do you take such a dim view of my profession?"

"Because I compare it with mine. Do you know how much work I have to get through on this place?"

"Tell me."

"To start with, get the weeds off the lawn. Then hoe the rose-beds and spray the roses against mildew and rust. Soak the gladioli. Tie the irises to canes, syringe the sweetpeas, plant half-hardy annuals."

"Is that all?"

"I haven't even begun. Transfer cyclamen sown last August to pots, trim hedges, spray apples and pears, logan-berries, peaches and plums and damsons. Tie sacking round apple and pear trunks against apple blossom weevils."

"Is that the lot?"

"No, it isn't. Plant Brussels sprouts, savoys and broccoli. Grow salad crops, peas and French beans. Sow chicory. Start picking herbs and –"

"All right – I've got the message," Christopher broke in. "But just as you don't only pull out weeds, I don't only stand at a counter. There are other sides to bookselling."

97

He paused and then continued in a reflective voice. "If a bookseller fell in love with a lady gardener, would you call that incompatibility?"

"Yes."

"Why?"

"Because he's inside and she's outside and never the twain shall meet."

"We meet."

"Only because you neglect your business."

She was making tomato sandwiches. She cut more bread and got plates out of a cupboard.

"How else can I get to know you?"

"By lunching with me, as you're doing now. By coming in sometimes to have a light dinner."

"Could you bear to see me more than you do now?"

It was a long time before she answered. Then:

"Yes," she said. "I could."

"Do you want to see me more than you do now?"

"Isn't that what's called a loaded question?"

"Yes, it is. Perhaps I'm not making it clear how much depends on your answer. Do you like me at all?"

This time, the silence was longer.

"Yes," she said at last.

"Have you any idea what I feel for you?"

"I don't want to know – yet." She gave him his plate and led the way out to the bench. "I want to keep things . . . I think impersonal is the word I want."

"What do you mean by impersonal?"

"Keeping off certain subjects. Talking about things in general. For example, where did you go to school?"

"That's not impersonal."

"It'll do. Eton? Harrow? Borstal?"

"No. A place called Hasley Grange, in Brighton, and then Winchester."

"My school was a Grange, too. In Folkestone. My father chose it. My mother wasn't interested."

"Did you like it?"

"Yes, but only because I was a weekly boarder."

"So was I, at my prep school. I thought it a great mistake. I wasn't a day boy and I wasn't a boarder – I was something undefined in between. It wasn't until I got to Winchester that I began to feel what you might call integrated. Were you always as pretty as you are now?"

"I've never changed much, if that's what you mean. Where was your home?"

"Huntingdon. My parents were out in Malaya for the whole of my father's working life. Then they came back to England – to settle, they said. But they never really settled. They roamed. When they'd finished with Scotland, they went round Wales. Then they had a season or two near Biarritz. When I say season, I mean out of season – they weren't exactly on the bread line, but they couldn't afford to spend seasons anywhere. They stayed in Huntingdon when I was on holiday from school and then they resumed their travels."

"Who looked after you?"

"Various aunts. I had four, all very peculiar."

"Married?"

"Widowed. One of them went round York on a tricycle with a little dog in the basket in front. Another one ran a pet shop in Deal. Numbers three and four lived together in a large house in Chester and held weekly meetings at which everyone sang glees and madrigals. Staying with them was never a boring experience."

"Are they still alive?"

"No. They died almost together – one, two, three, four, just like that. After that I was on my own. My parents had gone to live in a varied selection of the South Sea Islands. They're still there. They send postcards – very colourful, very uninformative."

"Don't they ever come to England?"

"No. They like heat and outdoor living – neither readily

99

available in this country. Besides which, their money goes further where they're living."

"Money . . ." Kathryn spoke in an absent tone.

"Yes, money. What you need to buy food and clothes and so on. Is it true that your mother's uncle has died?"

"Yes. Last week."

"That means that your mother will henceforth be rich?"

"She'll get his money, yes."

"So you'll be an heiress. That means that I must now spend more time than ever in this garden, pursuing you. But you must never forget that I pursued you in the days when you were poor. You must remember that my first stirrings of passion came when you were a bridesmaid in a lemon-coloured dress, and your hair . . ."

"Christopher, why do you always talk such rubbish?"

"It's all the vocabulary I possess. Do you realise that it's time you went out with me?"

"Do you realise it's a long time since you asked me?"

"I've been saving up. I could hardly ask you to come and share my dinner at Mrs. Preston's, could I?"

"You could spend more time in your shop, selling more books and earning more money."

"You've never been into the shop since I dropped the books on you. I keep hoping, but you never come. Don't you ever need a nice, improving book?"

"No."

"Just because you're an heiress?"

"I'm anything but. I'll never get any of my mother's money."

"Why not?"

"Because she regards what she's got as hers. She had an income of her own when she married my father, and it was agreed between them that she'd keep it for her own use. She took that literally. When he lost some of his money, she didn't come forward with any offer of help. The way she sees it, I suppose it's fair enough. I got my father's money when he died. It wasn't much, but my mother made it clear that that was all I'd ever get. It's a nice little addition to my earnings."

"What's she going to do with all that money of hers when she dies?"

"I've no idea. I don't want it – she knows that. So if you're looking for an heiress, you'd better put a notice in the bookshop window."

"Are you an only child?"

"Yes. Are you?"

"Yes. I never wanted brothers and sisters much."

"Neither did I. All the same, I'd like to have a large family when I marry."

He swallowed a mouthful of sandwich.

"Any idea when that'll be?" he asked.

"No. In the unforeseeable future."

"Why wait so long? Be careful – or you might find yourself on what I think they call 'the shelf' – or might it be the bookshelf?"

"How do you know I'm not one of those women who don't want to marry?"

"Easy. If you were, you wouldn't be spending time keeping George and Stella's garden in order. You'd be out there in the big world, sitting at an outsize desk in a plate-glass office, with three phones and five secretaries. You'd be planning to be the next woman Prime Minister. You wouldn't be living in a cottage like this one – you'd have one of those so-called cottages in the Home Counties, near enough to commute to your London office. You'd travel. Not a minor trip like George and Stella's, but world-wide. You'd have contacts in Bonn and Singapore and Tokyo. You'd . . . would it be all right if I cut myself another sandwich?"

"Why not biscuits and some of the nice Camembert I bought?"

"That sounds all right." He got up and went inside,

returning with two plates, both piled with biscuits and cheese.

"I'm enjoying my lunch," he said, re-seating himself beside her. "I can – and do – have sandwiches when I'm on my own, but whoever it was who said that two was company, made sense. Can I come again tomorrow?"

"No. My mother's coming down on a visit."

"Pity. Any idea how long she's staying?"

"She can't stand Crane for more than a week."

"Then why does she come?"

"She comes to find out what I'm doing. She likes to know what's going on."

"That shows a certain interest in your welfare, doesn't it?"

"No. She thinks I'm like my father – easy-going, unambitious, content to drift. She's frightened because she thinks that one day, I'll need help – financial help. That would mean that her friends would see that I'm due for a hand-out, and she wouldn't like their knowing that she's not prepared to give it. For years, she's tried to make me marry a man – any man – who has money. That would get me right off her mind."

"So she banked on Roach?"

"Yes."

"As we've touched on Roach, could I ask what the situation is? He still shows up at weekends. You seem to have stopped going round with him, but he's still – so to speak – a factor in the case. Is it just a quarrel?"

"No. I'm not going out with him any more. What's more –"

"What's more?"

"– I'm sorry I kept it up for so long."

"Can I take it that you're through?"

"You can. But telling my mother won't be easy."

"If I put our plates inside, could I demonstrate, by actions, just how glad I am?"

"No."

"Pity. I was just beginning to persuade myself that I was progressing. You can't say I'm an impatient man, can you?"

"I can and I do."

"Count it up. How many weeks since the wedding? It was at the wedding when my eyes fell on you in your bridesmaid's dress and I told myself I was a goner. Since then, I've been trying to get nearer to you, but I can't assess how far I've travelled." He put the plates on the bench beside him and turned to her. "Have I travelled at all?"

Her eyes went slowly round the lovely garden before them. She spoke with her eyes still on it.

"Yes," she said. "I think you can say you've travelled."

"Thank you." He dropped a kiss on her cheek. "That," he said, "is the first station on the route."

Mrs. Malden arrived two days later and, with some belittling remarks about its lack of comforts, settled herself into the spare bedroom of the cottage. Beyond arriving in a rented car, it did not seem to Kathryn that her forthcoming increase of fortune had as yet brought about any change in her life style. She told Kathryn that she was giving herself time to plan how she was going to live in future.

She made no reference to her recently deceased uncle, and gave Kathryn no indication of how much she expected to get from his estate. She paid a visit to George and Stella, was invited to stay for dinner, and did so. Stella's intention in not including Kathryn in the invitation was, as she explained to George, to give the combatants a brief breathing space.

"What you mean," he amended, "is that you want to give Kathryn a rest from her mother's carping."

"It comes to the same thing."

Mrs. Malden did not for the first two days make any

reference to Aubrey Roach. Her remarks were confined to
her own plans.

"I've begun to look round for a flat – in London. I don't
want a house."

"Are you selling –"

"– my uncle's? Yes."

"It's got a nice central position."

"But it's too big and too late-Victorian. I won't move out
of London. After life with your father, I never want to live
in the country again. I've got as far as putting a down-
payment on a nice place a stone's throw from Harrods." She
paused. "And what about you? Are you really going to stay
down here playing the lady gardener?"

"Yes. Why not? I don't like London and I like the
Deepleys and I like this town and I like my job."

"Is that the limit of what you want out of life?"

"At the moment, yes."

The legacy, Kathryn thought, had certainly not improved
her mother's disposition. There was the same open sarcasm,
the same scarcely-veiled contempt, the same irritation and
impatience she had shown her husband throughout their
married life. Once, not so long ago, Kathryn had asked her
mother why she had never left him.

"Security," Mrs. Malden had replied. "Not security in
the ordinary sense of the word. He provided a background.
I could do as I pleased, but I did it against a backcloth
of charming-woman-married-to-charming-man, with pretty
daughter. That gave me a sort of cachet, and I felt I needed
it. And for all his faults, he was an easy man to live with.
He didn't make demands and he didn't ask questions."

At breakfast on the third morning of her visit, Mrs.
Malden brought up the subject which Kathryn guessed had
been the reason for her visit. She helped herself to a second
cup of coffee and spoke carelessly.

"What," she enquired, "have you done to Aubrey
Roach?"

"Stopped going out with him."

Mrs. Malden said nothing for a time. Then she spoke slowly.

"My God, you're a fool. What were you thinking of?"

"Getting rid of him – by degrees. I didn't want to hurt him."

"Hurt! You sound like your father. Aubrey told me he wanted to marry you."

"He told me that, too."

"And you refused?"

"Yes."

"Being very careful not to hurt him?"

"Yes."

"So now what? Rumour has it that you're involved with a bookseller – that man called Hobart. Is it true?"

"No. There's no involvement."

"There must be. He's here, I've heard, day after day, following you round while you snip off roseheads. How you can let a catch like Aubrey Roach go, I can't understand. In fact, why you didn't grab him at the very beginning is beyond me. Now it looks as though you've left it too long. All you've got now is a backwater job – and whatever money you've got left out of your inheritance. I hope you don't imagine that you can call on me for any."

"No. You've always made the position very clear."

"Did you quarrel with Aubrey Roach?"

"No. I just told him I wasn't proposing to go out with him any more, that's all."

"All? And you think a man like him will hang around waiting for you to change your mind?"

"No. I don't care if I never see him again."

Mrs. Malden pushed her chair back from the table, and rose.

"Yes, fool's the word," she said. "I'm certain he bought

that cottage – what's it called? – Pond Cottage, so that he could settle here for weekends and see you. To let a man like him get away is madness. Can't you see that?"

"If I'm not in love with him, what point is there in letting him see me whenever he wants to?"

Mrs. Malden looked round for an ashtray and lit a cigarette.

"I give up," she said. "Your life is your life and you can ruin it if you want to. Now let's talk about something else. What did the Deepleys do when they went on that trip?"

"Didn't they tell you?"

"No. The conversation was exclusively of enamel jewellery and art clubs."

"They enjoyed it, but they lost some things when they were burgled just before they left. Stella lost a valuable brooch."

"Too bad. About the car. You're using it, but it belongs to me. I want a better one, so if you'd like to make a deal, you can keep it."

"Thank you, but no. I don't really need a car here. I've got my bike, and there's a good bus service, and if I need to go anywhere that's any distance away to buy seeds and so on, George will take me."

"A bike, a bus and a bookseller. The good life. Well, I came for a week, but if you don't mind, I think I'll cut it short. There's a lot for me to arrange in London. You can put the car on the market and send me the proceeds."

When she left, nobody was sorry to see her go. Christopher, who had kept away during her stay – to avoid, he told Kathryn, being insulted to his face – resumed his visits.

George, observing the two as he went about his work in the garden, saw easily enough what Christopher's feelings were regarding Kathryn, and wondered whether he had any hope of getting on to ground that had lately been the exclusive property of Aubrey Roach. He also wondered how

Aubrey Roach would react to a dismissal. He did not look like a man who would take it meekly.

It was some time before Aubrey called at the cottage. Two weeks went by, and Kathryn saw nothing of him. Then one morning she saw a large car drawing up outside the cottage, guessed it was his, and realised that the meeting was not going to be easy.

When she went in, he was standing beside the dining table. He looked slim, handsome and well turned out. For a moment she understood her mother and was fleetingly surprised that she herself had been able to see through this polished exterior to the very different man beneath.

Aubrey did not waste words.

"I didn't come before," he said, "because I wanted to give you time to think things over."

"Thank you. I didn't need time."

"No? You've been spending a good deal of it with that bookseller chap."

"His name's on the shop door – didn't you see it?"

"Hobart. Did you invite him to hang round you while you were working?"

"No. The Deepleys' garden isn't open to the public, but their friends can drop in if they want to."

"If he'd looked a more impressive fellow, I might have felt jealous – but he's no more than run-of-the-mill. I thought I'd give you time to get tired of him. That, at any rate, was the advice your mother gave me. Perhaps it wasn't as sound as I thought at the time. Does he monopolise all your leisure, or would you be interested in coming out with me? I'm testing a new car."

"What was the matter with the old car?"

"Superseded by this new model. I hope I haven't been superseded by a new model. Come out and take a look at it."

"No."

"Not interested in lunch? Dinner?"

"Thank you. No."

He leaned against a chair and studied her. His expression, at all times controlled, gave nothing away.

"That," he pointed out, "is the first time you've said no when I've suggested going somewhere."

She did not answer. She realised that in spite of having known him for so long, she knew little or nothing about his life. Her intermittent enquiries had been turned aside by a vague explanation that he was on the Stock Exchange, an occupation it was no use discussing with her. She was in no doubt, now, of what she was losing. He loved her. It would be, if she married him, the good life in the sense her mother had not used the expression. But she did not love him, had never loved him, and her days with Christopher had taught her what real companionship could be.

"I want to see you as I see other people," she told him. "I want to meet you some weekends but not every weekend. I want to be free to say no to you whenever I want to."

"As you said no when I asked you to marry me?"

"Yes."

"Left it a bit late, haven't you? It's over a year since I bought Pond Cottage with a view to seeing you. We had fun, didn't we?"

"Yes, we did. A lot. Thank you. But everything comes to an end."

He went towards the door.

"Well, remember one thing," he said. "I've got a hell of a lot more to offer you than that bookseller."

She would have liked to say that that bookseller had nothing to do with her decision. But it would not have been true. He had guessed it. Ken had guessed it. George and Stella had guessed it. All she could do was let him go, and hope that he would stay away. Life had taken a new turn.

George came in shortly after the car had left.

"Sorry to be nosey," he said, "but did you have a fight?"

"No."

"Still going out with him?"

"No."

"Good. I've nothing against him, but he's not my favour-ite man. Did you have difficulty in shaking him off?"

"Not much."

"Any regrets?"

"No."

"Good," George said, and went to give the news to Stella.

7

Stella was enjoying her morning visits to the hospital. It was a cottage hospital, built on a slight rise, with woodland at the back and neat lawns on the other three sides. Her contact with the convalescent patients was brief but friendly; sometimes she learned their names and guessed something about them from their taste in literature. It was disconcerting, and at times disappointing, to enter a ward and find that a familiar figure had been discharged and a stranger now occupied the bed.

She visited the kitchens and found them up to her own standard: spick and span, and efficiently run. She made friends with the doctors and nurses and was congratulated on her renewed stock of books. The visits lengthened imperceptibly until she began to reach home only just in time to prepare lunch for herself and George, and sandwiches for Ken.

June had brought almost unprecedented weather – days of hot sunshine, and evenings so mild and clear that George, Stella and Kathryn pooled their light dinners and carried them out to a table on the lawn. On some evenings, if George and Stella dined out, Christopher came to join Kathryn. She got up very early in the mornings, worked through the day and stopped early; then she went into the cottage, had a bath, changed and prepared dinner for two. Christopher thought that she looked, in her summer attire, even more desirable than she had been in her bridesmaid's outfit.

One evening, Stella brought out a piece of work.

"Knitting?" Kathryn asked in surprise.

"Trying to. In between painting and enamelling, I'm

trying to learn new tricks. Look." She held up the work. "My first attempt at a sweater for George."

There was a pause.

"Something," Christopher ventured, "seems to have gone wrong."

"Nothing's gone wrong except that I've dropped some stitches, and the pattern isn't coming out the way it looks in the picture. How d'you think I'm getting on, Katie?"

Kathryn, gazing at the snarl of wool, found herself unable to comment.

"I knew you'd say that." Stella rolled up the work despairingly.

"Why don't you make a start on something easier?" Christopher suggested. "For instance, a scarf."

"No, no scarves. I wanted to do something interesting. It looked easy, in the picture." She looked wrathfully at the work. "What can I use this for?"

"It would make a lovely kettle holder," Christopher said.

"I dare say. But what I'm going to use it for is garbage."

"Don't give up. You don't want George to catch cold, do you?" he asked.

"If it means doing any more knitting, the answer's yes."

When she had gone indoors, Christopher and Kathryn sat on to enjoy the slight breeze that had blown up. After a time, Ken joined them. He fetched a cup from the cottage, poured out the last of the coffee and drank it.

"Nice life," he commented. "Out in the fresh air all day and half the night. I like this job. A fine job for an orphan boy."

"You're not an orphan," Kathryn said. "Or are you?"

"As good as."

"You've got a mother. Don't you know where she is?"

"Yes, I know. She's in Vancouver. You know Vancouver?"

"Of course I know Vancouver."

"There's no 'of course' about it," said Ken. "When I was small, at school, none of the kids knew. One of 'em thought it was in India, and he asked his grandmum, who'd been in India when the British were running it, but he came back and said that all the names had been changed since the British got thrown out."

"The British were not thrown out," said Kathryn.

"All right, so they weren't."

"Doesn't your mother ever write to you or to your grandmother?"

"No. Not any more. Once she did, but then she stopped. My grandmum said she must be dead, but she wasn't dead. When she knew that, my grandmum said I ought to go out and live with her because she was too old to go on looking after me, specially the way I couldn't keep jobs. I might have gone, just for laughs, but my mother said no, it was better for me to be in England. So I didn't go, and when I met Maureen, I was glad I'd stayed here."

"What was your first job?" Kathryn asked.

"Doing all the heavy jobs in Maureen's father's shop. When he saw I was after Maureen, that was it. Out. He told everyone I was a drop-out, but that wasn't true. I've lost jobs, all right, but only because I got fed up with them and left them, not because I was sacked. At least, most of the time."

"You have to stick to jobs, even if you don't like them," Christopher told him.

"Why? A job is all day and every day. If there are people in it who like you, or who you like, or who treat you right, then you stay there. But if you're treated like mud, or if you don't like what you're doing, you quit."

"Well, I hope you like what you're doing now," Kathryn

said. "It might be a good idea if you got on with doing it."

"I'm only having a breather. Katie, have you ever taken a good look round this garden?"

"Of course I have."

"I don't mean the lawn and the vegetables and the flower-beds. I mean that part of it that's down below, on the lower part of the hill. Why doesn't Mr. Deepley do something with it? It'd make a nice rockery, or a lily pond or something. When I was little I used to play there all by myself. I used to throw pine cones on to the people who were walking along the lower road – the road that goes past the church to the old windmill. They couldn't see me. Up above it, at the top of the hill, there's Maureen's father's shop. Haven't you ever looked down there?"

"I've looked, but I've never really explored it," Kathryn said.

"Then why don't you come and look at it now?"

Kathryn hesitated.

"Would it take long?" she asked.

"'Course it wouldn't." Ken got to his feet. "Let's go. Coming, Chris?"

"Yes."

"From the bottom," said Ken, leading the way, "you can see the back entrance of the shop. Here we are. Careful how you go. It's a bit slippery in parts."

They were soon making their way through thick under-growth. It was hard going, and Kathryn had almost decided to turn back when Ken gave an exclamation.

"Man, look at that! Here's something that wasn't here last time I came down. Looks like . . . yes, it's a car. How could a car get here?"

She moved up to it to have a closer look and spoke in a tone of astonishment.

"Just look at the state it's in! Everything removable removed."

"How long would you say it had been here?" Christopher asked.

"Not so long," Ken said. "But like Katie said – everything taken away but the body-work."

Christopher was looking up to the top of the hill.

"It must have come over the edge of that path behind Willie Bolt's shed," he said. "Ken, do you remember hearing anything about an accident?"

"This was no accident." Ken was close to the abandoned car, bending over and examining it. He looked up through a clump of bushes. "Chris, look at that fence."

Christopher looked up. There was a wooden fence bordering Willie Bolt's property, and several boards had been removed, giving enough space for a car to pass through.

"See that?" Ken's tone had changed – it sounded eager. "Someone drove – no, not drove, shoved – this car over the edge of the hill down here to what they thought would be a hidden place." He fought a way through a thick bush. "I'm going to climb up there and take a look."

The other two watched him as he scrambled hand over hand up the low hill. He was out of sight for a time, and then he came down by leaps and rejoined them.

"The fence was opened," he said. "Just wide enough to push this car through."

"It's a big car," Christopher said. "And it was once a good one."

They examined what they could see of it. Then they turned away and began to make their way back to the cultivated part of the garden.

"What beats me," Ken stopped to get his breath, "is how Willie Bolt could see that damage to his fence and not make a big row about it."

"What beats *me*," Kathryn said, "is why the car was put there in the first place. Stolen?"

"Dunno." Ken wiped the perspiration from his forehead. "But I'm going to have a go at finding out. The nearest garage is that one I used to work in. I might try pumping some of the chaps to see if they know anything." He looked anxiously at Kathryn and Christopher. "You'll keep this to yourselves, won't you? I mean, you won't say we went down there?"

"Not if you don't want us to," said Kathryn.

"I don't. 'Specially to Maureen."

They fought their way with difficulty back to the level of the lawn.

"Why," Kathryn asked Ken, "are you getting so excited about this?"

"I've told you. If someone wanted to get rid of a car, and chose that place to shove it into, then it couldn't have been done without some help, or at any rate some know-how, from Willie Bolt."

"There's nothing criminal about dumping a car in undergrowth, is there?"

"It was dumped on private land. And it wasn't dumped openly."

"But if there was anything underhand about it, wouldn't Willie Bolt have mended his fence?"

"Not necessarily. If he was paid to help, maybe there was going to be more pay for more dumping."

"Dumping the car on George's land," Christopher commented, "was hardly a friendly act."

"I keep telling you," Ken insisted. "It's got a smell of fish all over it. I'm going to wait a few days, and then I'm going down to take another look at that car to see if I can find out anything."

"And if you do, what are you going to do about it?" Christopher asked.

"Do? I don't know – but there's definitely something fishy about it. I'd like to find out how it got down there, because I've got a hunch that if there's any dirty dealing going on, Maureen's dad is in it up to his neck. If I could find out how and why, then —"

"Then what?"

"Then I'd have something to say about it to Willie Bolt if he ever got on my back again."

8

On a breezy morning two days later Stella, answering a ring on the doorbell, found herself confronted by Oliver Anvil.

"Oliver!" She gave a cry of welcome. "Where have you sprung from? Come in."

He followed her into the large, newly decorated drawing room.

"Not from Naples. From Bath," he told her. "How are you and George?"

"George and I are fine. He's working in the garden – I'll call him."

She went to a window and called. George appeared on the edge of the lawn.

"I'm busy," he called back. "Is it anything important?"

"It's Oliver Anvil."

George, as pleased as his wife had been to see the visitor, hurried indoors.

"What are you doing in this part of the world?" he asked.

"The fact is" – Oliver took the comfortable chair Stella indicated – "I'm homeless. I lived for a number of years in a furnished house in Bath. The lease came to an end, and I've been looking round trying to decide where to move to. Meeting you in Naples gave me the idea of seeing whether there was anywhere in Crane I could settle for a time. I found a new hotel called the Spire, so I checked in – and then came along to look you up."

George was looking doubtful.

"The Spire's impressive-looking," he said, "but they get a lot of doubtful customers. And it's expensive."

"It's comfortable, and the doubtful customers won't worry me much." He leaned foward to look out of a window.

"Who's the pretty girl in the garden? I thought all your daughters were married."

"They are. She's our gardener – and a good one," George said. "She lives in the gardener's cottage. She and her mother came here to start a dress shop, but it never got on its feet. Kathryn – the girl you're looking at – stayed here and became our gardener."

"Lucky you." Oliver leaned back in his chair. "What happened to the mother?"

"She went to London, to live with an old uncle who's since died."

"She's a widow?"

"Yes. Her uncle left her enough to keep her very comfortable."

"Who was he?"

"Woodham, of Woodham Enterprises," George answered. Oliver whistled.

"Very comfortable is right," he said. "Is she as pretty as her daughter?"

"Yes – but she hasn't got her daughter's nice disposition," Stella said. "She looks pretty until she can't get her own way, but if she's crossed, she turns into a cat."

"That happens to a number of women I know," Oliver said.

George was getting out drinks.

"Tell me, have you done any travelling since we saw you last?" he asked.

"Not much. I spent a few weeks in Paris. I like Paris at this time of the year. By the way, did you ever hear any more about those things of yours that were stolen in Naples?"

"Not one word," said Stella in disgust.

"I didn't think you would. 'See Naples and be robbed' would be a more accurate rendering of the old saying. Just after you left, one of the friends I was staying with was backing his car down a street. He turned to see where he was going, and his watch – a valuable one – was snatched off his wrist."

"Naples hasn't got a monopoly of the snatching racket," George commented. "It's pretty widespread now."

"You're right." He smiled at Stella. "I can't stay long," he told her. "I just dropped in to say I'm here and that I hope to see a lot of you both. Perhaps you'll let me sample some of your famous cooking?"

"I'll give a dinner party and invite some people to meet you," Stella promised.

"Thank you." He took the drink George handed him. "What I find so extraordinary," he went on, "is the way Outercrane has outstripped its older sister. It didn't exist when my grandfather first came here, but now it's well ahead of Crane in everything but size. Its streets are wider, its shops are more up-to-date, and that shopping complex is well done – free from traffic, and with flower boxes along it, and benches for people to rest on."

"Crane just grew," said George. "Outercrane is the result of town planning."

"That's true. And the fact that there's no way out of it except the way you've come in has kept it to a reasonable size. Is there any more room for development?"

"There's land for sale," George answered. "But the price is pretty steep."

"I'd like to take a look at it," Oliver told him. "I'd consider it a good investment. What I really want to do," he went on, "is find a place I can settle in. Many people – people who can afford it – buy a house in London and a cottage in the country. I used to feel that that was the wrong way round – live in the country, I thought, and go up to London to work. But lately, I've changed my mind. I've seen some flats for sale in London that are the latest thing in comfortable living. I've got my eye on one of them."

Something about the casual way in which he spoke confirmed George's impression – formed in Naples – that he was a man of means.

"I noticed," Oliver was saying, "that there was no building down by the river. I suppose that's because it's liable to flood."

"Yes. Floods are a regular spring event here," George said.

"I remember them well. No, I won't have another drink, thanks." He rose. "I must be going. I'll come and tell you how I get on with the house-hunting."

When he had driven away, Stella followed George into the garden.

"That was a fellow we met in Naples," George told Kathryn. "Name of Anvil. He used to live in Crane when he was a boy. He's a nice fellow. You'll like him."

Stella was frowning.

"Will you tell me," she asked, "what it is about rich bachelors that irritates me?"

"I can answer that," said George. "You want to hitch them up to nice girls who're looking for husbands."

"I suppose that's it. What I feel is that if there's a good deal of money – which in this case is obvious – then there ought to be a family to share it with. Instead of talking about comfortable flats in London, Oliver ought to be moaning about the rise in school fees or the cost of summer holidays, as you used to do. Don't you remember what you had to pay when the girls went with the school skiing group to Switzerland?"

"I remember what it cost to marry them off. Three dowries in three years. And their clothes! My God, their clothes! And all they ever said was that they had nothing to wear. Nothing to wear? Did you ever see them in the same outfit two weeks running?"

"Girls need nice clothes," said Kathryn.

"They weren't nice clothes. They were garments of the kind that used to be worn at carnivals. There wasn't a decent dress or a neat suit among them. They always looked to me as though they'd bought the things off second-hand stalls."

"Some of their friends did – and do," said Kathryn.

"And boots. Stomping round the house wearing cowboy boots. And that hair! As soon as you'd got used to seeing it cut short, it reappeared in the form of Medusa's locks."

"All they did was follow the fashions," Stella told him.

"I know. But fashions," George told Kathryn, "used to be set by women in the upper social strata, and were copied by the herd. When our girls – and when you – were growing up, it was the other way round. Now it's the young who set the styles."

"And your young," Stella reminded him, "had to work hard to get you to part with money for the styles."

"And you were invariably on their side. As you're in the garden, why don't you do some weeding?"

"No. I pull up the wrong things."

"Katie and I will replant them for you, won't we, Katie? Come on – it's good exercise."

During the weeks that followed, George and Stella saw a good deal of Oliver. He was busy looking for accommodation in Crane, and he was soon to have some help in the search. Stella, giving the promised dinner party, invited Mr. Vernon, Mrs. Woodley and the Harleys, and decided to ask Mrs. Malden to come down from London to make the numbers even. Oliver gave his attention to all the guests impartially, but something told Stella that he was planning to see more of Kathryn's mother. She was proved right when the two went on with the house-hunting together.

"He's fallen for her," George guessed. "Not that it means anything. A man doesn't get to his age as a bachelor without having escaped a few matrimonial traps."

"Where's the trap?" Stella wanted to know. "She doesn't want a man. With all her money –"

"Oh yes, she does. Not any man. But a man like Anvil – a sophisticated, experienced man of the world, well-informed, presentable – she'd take him if he was on offer. Which somehow I don't think he is."

"Sometimes you verge on the cynical, do you know that? You used to talk like that about Aubrey Roach. I never could make out exactly what you had against him."

"Too smooth. And selfish as hell. I never considered him husband material. And he was too cagey for my liking. Who knows what he did in London during the week? He might have been keeping a woman there. Even a wife."

"What wife would have let her husband go away every weekend?"

"I don't know. But I always thought there was something fishy about Roach, and I don't mean only his name."

There was nothing fishy about Oliver Anvil. Both George and Stella found him unfailingly good-humoured, easy of manner, considerate and amusing. He was welcomed in Crane by everyone who had known or heard of his grandfather. He made friends wherever he went – and wherever he went, Mrs. Malden now went with him. She came down frequently from London, but she did not stay with Kathryn at the cottage; she stayed at the Spire Hotel. Oliver was still living there, ignoring all George's criticisms of its drawbacks and its undesirable clientele.

Christopher had by now established the habit of walking to the Deepleys' garden every morning. If he had failed to arrive, Kathryn realised, she would have found something missing in the day. She noted that on his arrival, George invariably found work to do in some other part of the garden.

"Since you spend so much time here," she said to Christopher one morning, "why don't I make some use of you?"

"Give me a job to do, you mean?"

"Yes."

"Could I talk to you while I was doing it?"

"Not necessarily."

"Then let's go on the way we're going. Unless, of course, there's something I can do to save you doing it."

"That's the idea. You could start by lifting the spring bulbs that have turned yellow. They ought to be put into shallow boxes and dried in the shed."

"I'll tell Ken to see to it. Anything else?"

"The lawn needs spiking to let the water penetrate."

"Fine. He shall spike the lawn."

"The primroses need dividing for replanting. And the border carnations need staking."

"And if I did any of those things, I wouldn't be able to talk to you."

"That's true," she admitted.

Ken came to join them.

"We were just discussing some jobs you could do," Christopher said. "Incidentally, how's the detective work going?"

"It isn't going." Ken sounded gloomy. "Nobody round here has ever heard of a car being stolen."

"Why does it have to be round here?" Kathryn asked.

"Stands to reason. Anyone trying to hide a stolen car – and I'll bet that one down there is stolen – wouldn't want to take it far before stripping it and dumping it. So they couldn't have been far from Willie Bolt's shop. One thing's certain – Bolt was in the know. If he hadn't been, like I said before, he'd have gone round screeching about the damage to his fence. One of the guys at the garage where I worked said he'd heard, or thought he'd heard, something about a car that had gone missing from a place about eight miles from here. I'm going to follow it up. It's not much to go on, but you have to start somewhere."

"What makes you so keen on finding out?" Kathryn asked.

"I told you. Because I'm sure that Willie Bolt had a hand in it. I don't say I'd give him away if I found he was mixed up in anything – in fact, I wouldn't be able to, on account of Maureen – but I could give him a kind of hint that I'd found out something, and then he'd have to stop calling me names and he'd have to let me go out with Maureen – in the open, like, not the way we see each other now. It's worth a try."

Kathryn agreed, and looked at her watch. It was lunchtime. She had invited Christopher to a snack meal. Now she included Ken.

"Mrs. Deepley left me some sandwiches," he explained.

"Then go and get them and join us."

They met at the cottage.

"Cold chicken and cheese and drinks," Kathryn said. "And that's all."

"I'll throw in my sandwiches," Ken said. "Look – cheese and tomato, sardines, peanut butter." He took a large bite out of one. "Seen your mum lately?" he asked Kathryn with his mouth full.

"No."

"It's none of my business, but she and that Mr. Anvil have got pretty chummy. A good pair, they are – meaning that they're both good lookers."

"He's advising her about buying a new car," Kathryn told him.

"You won't get much for that old rattle-trap you're trying to sell."

"I know that." Kathryn had put plates and glasses and food on the table. "Come and get it – if," she added as Ken bit into the second sandwich – "you haven't already got it."

"What," Ken asked Kathryn, "did your mum do before you came here to start that dress shop?"

"Ran a bridge club."

"And what were you doing?"

"I was finishing my third year at London University. She and I didn't live together. We tried it when I graduated, but it didn't work. She lived in a two-bedroom flat which didn't fit us both – and she was always entertaining her bridge friends, and I just seemed to get in the way. So I moved out and took a room near Cromwell Road. Then I did a course at a horticultural college. I liked living on my own – still do, actually."

"What made your mother come down here in the first place?" Christopher asked.

"One of her bridge friends said there was an opening for a new dress shop in Crane. My mother was quite sure she could make a success of it. She gave up her bridge club and asked me to come down here and help her to get started. But the thing folded. I didn't want to go back to London and look for a job – I was longing to do something out in the open. I'd got my diploma from the college, so I asked Mr. Deepley if he'd give me the job of gardener. He'd just had his heart attack and it was obvious that he couldn't manage the garden alone, even with you doing the heavy digging. He said he'd take me on, so here I am."

She got up to put the kettle on for coffee.

"And now you," Ken said to Christopher.

"Me? What is this, an interrogation?"

"Yes. I like to be entertained while I eat." Ken bit heartily into a chicken leg. "What were you doing before you started selling books?"

"Travelling, mostly. Then I got a history scholarship to Cambridge."

"Don't you ever want to go on travelling, get out of a town, get into the open, get away from the shop?"

"Sometimes. I keep a small boat at Newhaven, but I've been too busy to do much sailing lately." He turned to Kathryn. "Do you like sailing?"

"I haven't done any since my father died."

"Did he have a boat?"

"A small one. I used to like going out in it. He and I got on in a way my mother and I never could. He was quiet, but he was . . . well, he was fun-loving."

When the kettle boiled, she made coffee and they carried their cups to a window-seat. Outside, the garden looked beautiful, resplendent with colour. They could hear bird song, but otherwise it was tranquil.

"I'm enjoying this," Christopher said.

"So am I," said Ken. "But if I don't get back to work, Katie'll report me to the boss."

"I'm your boss," she said.

"No, you're not. You're the foreman. Remember to tell Mr. Deepley that I went back to the job before even cleaning up the chicken bones."

When he had gone, Christopher made more coffee. There was a long, comfortable silence until Christopher voiced a puzzled question.

"What was it," he asked, "that got you into the habit of going out at weekends with Roach?"

She took a long time to answer.

"At first," she explained at last, "it was just an occasional outing. Then he began to ring me up and fix weekend dates. After that, I drifted into what you've just called it – a habit. But there was always something unreal about the situation. I never knew what he did when he was away from this place. If I ever asked, he said something vague about the Stock Exchange and then talked about something else. All I knew was that he had a flat in Brook Street – and a lot of friends. I don't know why I always thought of the friends as the kind of people who patronise the Spire Hotel. He used to meet a number of them there."

"Did he take you?"

"No."

Silence fell again. When he spoke, it was in a different tone.

"Do you ever," he asked, "think about that bookseller who fell in love with a bridesmaid?"

"Yes. But –"

"But?"

"I said just now that I didn't know anything about Aubrey Roach. But when you come to think of it, how much do I know about you? I see you every day in the garden. I know some facts about your life – but can one really fall in love on that basis?"

"One can, and one does. I love you. Do I need to say it again? I love you very much – right down, deep down inside me. I haven't any doubts about how I feel about you. I want to marry you and settle down here in Crane or Outercrane with you. It's not a bad place to live. I haven't much money, but there's a good chance of making a real success of the shop. Could you ever consider me as a husband?"

She did not reply for some time.

"Well?" Christopher asked at last.

"I like you – a lot."

"That's not enough."

"I know. But I feel it's too soon to –"

He put his arms round her and laid his lips on hers. Then he freed her.

"Somehow," he said, "I'd hoped – I don't know why – that you felt about me as I felt about you. I obviously jumped to the wrong conclusion."

She looked up at him. She knew that it was not a wrong conclusion. She felt about him as she had never felt about any man before. She wanted to keep him beside her. She wanted to listen to his quiet voice with the humorous undertones. She wanted him to take her again into his arms.

"Christopher –" she began.

"It's all right. You need time," he said.

"No, I don't. I mean, I don't need time to decide what I think about you. All I need is time to realise, to believe, that I could fall in love with a man I met such a short time ago. Falling in love means putting aside everybody who up to now has been part of one's life. It means that one person matters more than anybody else."

"And you're not ready to put me first?"

"I don't think so. You mean more to me than all the

others put together, but the idea's too new to – to believe in."

"I love you," he said again. His tone was quiet and even. "I love you very much. If I kiss you – like this – will it help you to accept the situation?"

"Yes. But –"

"Another but?"

"What I'd like, if it's all right with you, is to go on as we are now."

"You mean we don't let anybody know that we're more than friends?"

"Yes, that's what I mean. I love you. I don't know how it's happened, but it's happened and I know, as you know about your own feelings, that they're deep. But I feel it's too early to –"

"– let the facts get around?"

"Yes. Most people have guessed. My mother would have made things difficult if she hadn't found Oliver Anvil to go around with and take her mind off me."

"Where can we meet to be alone?"

"Here in this cottage."

"When?"

"Whenever you want. Will you agree to keep it all to ourselves – for a little while?"

"Yes," he said – and no more. For the moment, it was enough.

9

On a warm, sunny morning a few days later, Stella carried two cups of coffee out to the garden, gave one to Kathryn and settled herself on a garden bench to talk.

"If it's not prying," she said without preamble, "I'd like to know what your reactions are about your mother going round with Oliver Anvil."

Kathryn joined her on the bench and sipped coffee. She seemed in no hurry to reply.

"I think I agree with Ken," she said at last.

"What's his opinion?"

"That they're a good pair."

"If she took it into her head to buy a house or a flat here, would you live with her?"

"No, never."

"Thank God for that. We couldn't do without you. Do you know that your mother and Oliver are now looking for an unfurnished place for him?"

"Yes. I think that's a sensible idea. She's good at interior decorating. She'll make it look nice."

"Sometimes I feel guilty because George and I kept such a large house for ourselves. It's a pity that when he designed it, he didn't give less thought to making rooms enough for a large family, and more to a future in which the family would have flown. We wanted more than three children. We'd settled for half a dozen – three of each – but that's not the way things turned out. I stopped at three girls, and nothing ever got me going again."

"You couldn't know that all three would go so far away when they married."

"That's true. It's such a pity that there's no hope of any

grandchildren growing up in this house. Later on, I suppose the children, if any, will be sent to school in England. Not the Australia and New Zealand children, but the Mozambique ones. If they come, they'll probably spend their holidays with us. But that's looking a long way ahead. Oh, I forgot. I've something to show you."

She groped in the pocket of her skirt and produced a short length of crochet for Kathryn's inspection.

"What does this look like to you?" she asked.

Kathryn looked at it doubtfully.

"I don't . . . I can't exactly . . ."

"You can't guess? Nor could anybody else. It's my attempt to do some bedsocks for charity. I don't know what went wrong, but somebody would have to have very odd feet to get them into this effort. I tried making squares for blankets, but they didn't come out square and they didn't come out the same size." She sighed and put the wool back into her pocket. "What I really came out to tell you," she went on, "is that it's Mr. Vernon's poetry reading this evening. Are you coming?"

"Do I have to?"

"No, you don't. But George and I have to. It's a yearly penance."

"As bad as that?"

"Almost. You needn't go if you don't want to, but George and I go because we feel sorry for him."

"Do many people turn up?"

"He fills the first four or five rows."

"And how many rows are there altogether?"

"About thirty."

"Can't he read poetry in a smaller hall?"

"He tried that. The number of listeners remained the same, only less spread out. Well, will you come? He'd be really pleased."

"Is it good poetry?"

"Mr. Vernon thinks so. I don't understand much of it,

and George goes into a doze. Coffee in the intervals, made and served by Miss Minter in a lacy apron. And Mrs. Woodley sings. Not well, I'm sorry to say."

"How much are the tickets?"

"It's a free show. That's to say, it's by invitation only. You should have got a card."

"I remember now, I did. I glanced at it and put it on the mantelpiece and forgot all about it." She paused to reflect. "Yes, I'll come. Can I go with you and George?"

"Of course. Six fifteen's zero hour. Meet you on the drive."

The annual poetry reading took place in the Crane Concert Chamber. It was a sunny evening which might have tempted people to stay out of doors, but the usual number of Mr. Vernon's supporters assembled before half past six.

The first reading, ten years earlier, had been an ambitious affair held in the town hall, but, as only a sparse audience was present, Mr. Vernon had wisely lowered his sights and now held the readings in a smaller and more intimate building. No entrance fee was asked, but there were two intervals during which coffee and biscuits were served, and for these a charge was made.

Though this year's attendance was as poor as it had been in previous years, Mr. Vernon showed no signs of disappointment, remaining at the entrance to shake the hands of all comers. The arrangements for the reading were simple: on the stage stood a piano, an elegant piano stool, a chair and a small table on which were a glass, a flask of water and the poet's manuscripts, together with the book of verse which had been published some years earlier.

Not only poetry was offered. At the first reading, Mr. Vernon had felt that it would be a good idea to provide a musical item between the poems, and had asked Mrs. Woodley – who had once sung in the chorus of an opera company – if she would sing three songs, one during each of the three scenes. She had agreed with alacrity. She accompanied herself on the piano, and for the first two or three years all had been well; if her voice was not, as Mrs. Truedom expressed it, anything to write home about, it was not unpleasant. But each year's rendering had shown a lamentable falling-off in tone and pitch, and it was only Mr. Vernon's reluctance to hurt her feelings that kept her name on the programme.

Oliver Anvil received an invitation to this year's reading, but as George predicted, found that urgent business called him elsewhere. This was a pity, for he was by now well known and respected in the town and his presence, George thought, might have induced others to attend. As it was, the first few rows were occupied by those who had occupied them at previous readings. Miss Minter sat at the end of a row, ready to slip out and prepare the coffee. Miss Grail helped her by collecting the payment. She came yearly, claiming to be a judge of poetry and willing to explain Mr. Vernon's to anybody who was not.

This year she had chosen to bring with her one of her dogs – a beautiful but not as yet fully trained puppy.

"It's quite all right," she assured the doubtful Mr. Vernon. "He's not coming inside. I'll tie him outside and he'll be as good as gold."

The reading began – not punctually, as Mr. Vernon always hoped that some latecomers might arrive. When it was clear that five rows was all he could hope to fill, he went behind the stage, rang a handbell and then, parting the curtains, walked to the table and stood bowing his acknowledgment of the polite applause. Then he sat, shuffled his manuscripts, cleared his throat and began the introductory speech that was unvaried year after year.

"I am very glad to welcome you all. I hope very much that you will enjoy what I am going to read to you. I am going to begin with one of my published poems. After that, I shall read you some of the poems which I have composed during the year." He gave a slight, conciliatory smile. "Two of them, you may think, dwell perhaps too much on the violent events that shadow our civilisation, but others are lighter in tone." He paused for a reshuffle. "The first poem I shall read is called 'Hasten'."

"'Hasten, oh hasten to –'"

He stopped. From the porch had come a heart-rending howl.

"Miss Grail –" he peered down at her "– perhaps you would very kindly –"

Miss Grail was on her feet.

"So sorry. I'll go and quieten him down."

The poet and his audience waited until the quietening-down process had been completed. Only when Miss Grail had resumed her seat did Mr. Vernon resume the reading.

"'Hasten, oh hasten
    To bind the cords of friendship ere they –'"

An even more heart-rending howl stopped him. Miss Grail, pink with mortification, hastened to the door, returning with the puppy, which she placed beside her.

"So sorry. He'll be all right now," she said.

The puppy settled down contentedly, and made no sound while Mr. Vernon declaimed. But no sooner had Mrs. Woodley struck a chord on the piano than he sat upright and gazed fixedly at the singer. As she uttered the first note, he gave vent to a prolonged wail that – Mrs. Truedom asserted later – put her in mind of a banshee.

It was impossible for the singer to proceed. Miss Grail, pinker than ever, called to Mr. Vernon that she must take the puppy home. Before she left, however, there was a delay while she handed the task of collecting payment for the coffee over to Mrs. Russell. When calm had been restored, Mrs. Woodley gave a rendering of 'Down in the Forest Something Stirred' – but the audience had become restive. Even after the second interval, when Mr. Vernon read them in an impassioned manner a poem entitled 'Deadly Night', it was clear that the life had gone out of the gathering.

At the end Mr. Vernon descended from the stage and joined the audience, and general sympathy was expressed for the marring of the performance. Mr. Vernon, however, seemed in no way put out. He went through the annual routine of wiping his brow, sighing with exhaustion and pressing the hands outstretched to his.

Stella, on the way home with George and Kathryn, wondered if there would be any future readings.

"There might," George said. "He'll have to put 'No Dogs Allowed' on his invitations."

"Hasn't there ever been any more interest in his performances?" Kathryn asked.

"Never," George answered. "This town never graduated beyond 'The Charge of the Light Brigade'. I read somewhere that the audiences don't really matter much. As long as two or three are gathered together, the reader's desire for listeners is satisfied. That was a beautiful dog, wasn't it? I wonder if –"

"We don't want any more," Stella said firmly. "We've got two."

"A nice little fellow like that could act as guard for Kathryn in the cottage."

"You mean he could be all my own?" Kathryn asked.

"All your own."

"Is he for sale?"

"Assuredly. All Miss Grail's animals are for sale. Want him?"

"I'd love him."

"He doesn't like singing."

"I won't sing."

She came in for a drink, and then refused dinner and walked back to the cottage. Shortly after she left, Oliver and Mrs. Malden appeared.

"Too late for a drink?" Oliver enquired.

"Never too late for a drink," George told him. "Come in, both of you."

They came in. Mrs. Malden was looking very attractive in a simple blue summer dress that matched her eyes.

"I'm sorry I missed out on the poetry reading," Oliver said, settling down in a chair. "But it wasn't really my line of country."

"Nor mine," George said. "But I've got a kind heart. I feel sorry for the poor poet."

Mrs. Malden leaned forward in her chair, and began to talk in her rather high but musical voice.

"We've come," she said, "to ask you both a favour. Before we tell you what it is, I'd like to say that it was my idea. If Oliver had ever thought of it, he hadn't mentioned it, I suppose because he felt it was asking too much."

"What is it?" Stella asked.

"It's this: as you know, Oliver and I have been looking for somewhere he can live. We almost settled on a place – but it turned out to be too cold and too sunless. We'd all but given up – and then I remembered that there was a wing of your house where you used to put up your daughters and their friends. I told Oliver about it and I brought him here this evening to see if you'd let him look over it and if it's suitable to you and to him let him rent it for a time. I told him it was beautifully furnished, with a nice combined drawing and dining room, and two bedrooms."

"But only a miniature kitchen," said George. "Nobody who stayed there ever had to cook."

"I know that." Mrs. Malden's tone became more animated. "That's what makes the whole idea such a good one. All Oliver needs is that little kitchen where you told me the girls used to make tea or coffee. Why can't you let him rent the flat, with Stella cooking dinner for him every evening? She wants someone to cook for, and she'd cook the kind of food that Oliver would appreciate. He wouldn't need lunch. If he was at home, he'd have a sandwich – otherwise he'd lunch out with friends."

Nobody spoke for a time, but on Stella's face could be

seen signs that the proposal had appealed to her. George broke the silence.

"Before going any further," he said, "the thing to do is show Oliver the rooms."

They went out of the drawing room, along a wide corridor, across a small hall, and then George opened the door to a sun-filled living room. Through this were two bedrooms, a bathroom and a small kitchen. The inspection over, they stood in the living room and Oliver spoke.

"It's too good to be true," he said with obvious sincerity. "I'd be – well, happy doesn't quite cover it. It's all I want. If you could find me a servant – a man, not a woman – to look after me, it would make the thing perfect. That is, if you agreed to my renting it."

"It's true," George said, "that Stella would enjoy producing dinner for you ever night. It could be sent over to you – I'd like this arrangement to be one which keeps us separate."

"So would I," said Oliver. "But finding a valet might be difficult – any kind of help is almost impossible to get here, I'm told."

They went back to the drawing room.

"Kathryn's mother isn't the only one who's got ideas," George said. "I think I've got a good one." He looked at his wife. "How about Ken taking over the job?" he asked.

"Ken's got a job," she said.

"I know he has. But he hasn't got a job that would prevent him from putting in a few hours looking after Oliver."

"All I need," Oliver said, "is someone to come in during the day to keep an eye on my clothes, and bring me my dinner. And of course keep the rooms clean."

"His grandmother would do that," Stella said.

"It's only fair to tell you," George went on, "that this young fellow – Ken – has had a number of jobs, and was thrown out of them all, but not for any – what shall I say? – misdemeanour. He just gets restless. I took him on full time in the garden for the summer, but if he gives you a few hours a day, he'll still be able to put in time doing some heavy work for me."

"I'd rather have someone like him working in the house," Stella said. "We've known him since he was a little boy."

"Could we sound him out?" Oliver asked.

"Yes," said Stella. "I think he'd take the job like a shot. But if this arrangement's going to work, I want a free hand. You can tell me if there's any food you particularly dislike, but otherwise I want to do the planning. I'll have your dinner ready on the minute – eight thirty – and Ken can come and fetch it and take it over to you. Is that agreed?"

It was agreed, and so were the terms on which Oliver could rent the wing. He was seen to the door by the Deepleys, and took Mrs. Malden away with him.

When they had finished their dinner that evening, George and Stella walked over to the cottage and told Kathryn the news.

"It'll bring a bit of life back into the house," George said. "You know it hasn't been easy for Stella, listening to what she calls echoes. I never minded for myself, but she had to learn the hard way what life's like when all the fledglings have left the nest. Do you think Ken would take on the job?"

"I'm not sure." Kathryn sounded doubtful. "You can ask him."

But to George's surprise, Ken opposed the offer.

"Not my style," he objected. "I'm no valet. I wouldn't be much good at cleaning and pressing his clothes and what not. I don't say he wouldn't be all right to work for – he seems a gent. And the pay's good, I'll say that." He gave a laugh. "Bit of a joke, me acting as a gentleman's gentleman."

"Give it a try," George urged. "You wouldn't have to get there until nine in the morning, and you can put in your free hours in the garden. After you've taken Mr. Anvil his dinner, you're free to go home."

"Will you at least talk to Mr. Anvil?" Stella asked.

It was a brief talk. Oliver's pay offer proved too good to turn down. When Ken informed his grandmother of the new arrangement, she gave a contemptuous sniff.

"You're going down 'ill," she told him. "All it is, you're going into service, same's I did. You can call it what you like, but you're just a domestic now. Still, you won't stick it for long."

In spite of this pessimistic forecast, the arrangement went well. Ken was given a new suit to wear while working in the house, and set about learning something of his new employer's ways. Dinner was wheeled over punctually at eight thirty, and the empty dishes taken back by Ken and put into Stella's dish-washer. There was no communication between the separate parts of the house unless Oliver came round by the front door to speak to George or Stella. His most frequent visitor was Kathryn's mother.

"Anything going on there, d'you think?" George asked his wife.

"I wouldn't be surprised. But it's not our business."

"Has Kathryn ever said anything about it?"

"Not to me. Come to think of it, it isn't her business either. Her mother's free and can take care of herself."

"Have you ever discovered what Oliver does for a living – if anything?"

"He's started up an office in London like the one he had in Bath – whatever that was. Some kind of financial set-up."

Ken told Christopher rather more than this.

"It's all money, money, money," he said. "His letters are beginning to come to the house now, and I see what's printed on the envelopes. He's got an office in Fenchurch Street and he goes up there three mornings a week. But what he does when he's there, I can't tell you."

Kathryn put the matter differently, and with some uneasiness.

"He's one of those financial wizards," she told Christopher. "He's given money by his clients and returns it to them – so he told my mother – sevenfold."

"Why does that worry you?"

"Because he might want to use some of mother's, and I think she ought to know much more about him before she lets him lay his hands on any."

"He's got a good background. The family was well thought of when they lived here."

"That was a long time ago. Who knows what they've been doing since then?"

Mrs. Malden was almost invariably with Oliver Anvil, and the townspeople spent much of their time speculating on the relationship between the two.

"If they asked me," Ken told Christopher one night, "I could spill a lotta beans. He's taken to letting me off early while they – he says – go out to dinner. D'you want to know something?"

"Yes."

"Well, I'll tell you. I like him a lot less than I did when I first went to work for him."

"Why?"

"I couldn't say, not for sure. It's the same feeling I've always had about Maureen's dad – that on top he's one thing, and underneath, he's something else. Something different." He frowned. "I'd give a lot to know how much Willie Bolt knows about that car that was driven or pushed through his fence."

"Still playing at being a detective?"

"Yeah. Haven't got far."

"Keep trying."

Ken eyed him.

"You're pretty sure I won't find out anything, aren't you?"

"I don't know. But I'll go as far as to say that I'm pretty sure there's something to find out."

Oliver had made no mention of Kathryn's mother's plans to buy a new car. But one day she drove up to the gardener's cottage in one that made Kathryn's eyes widen.

"Like it?" her mother enquired, still at the wheel.

"It's beautiful. But . . . isn't it too big?"

"Compared with the bathchair I had last, then yes, it's too big. But it's what I want. I drove very slowly on the way here, so that people could take a good look at it. They all went green with envy. I went round purposely by that Russell cat's mansion, to make sure she saw it too. Do you know what I paid for it?"

"Well, how much?"

When Mrs. Malden told her, Kathryn grew pale.

"You needn't look like that," her mother said. "I'd have had to give a lot more if I hadn't bought it through Oliver. I'm going to ask George if he'll let me have that garage he isn't using. I can leave this car in it whenever I'm out in Oliver's." She got out of the car. "Fix it with George, will you, and run the car in for me. I'm going in to see Oliver."

George was willing enough to let her have the unused garage. Kathryn drove the new car into it, and when Christopher came, she took him to see it. She also told him the cost, and he stood looking at it for a time in silence.

"Well, she can afford it," he said at last.

She was bending over one of the back wheels.

"Christopher, come and look," she said. "Can you see a mark on the wheel?"

"No."

"Look again. It's on the hub. As I passed the bushes that separate the cottage from the garden, I just brushed one of them with the back wheel. Can you see a mark?"

He bent to look.

"If you used a magnifying glass, you could see a kind of scratch. Is that what you mean?"

"I hope my mother won't see it."

"Not in a thousand years." He laughed. "It's just a scratch, but it's in the form of your initials. Look." He traced the mark with a forefinger.

"Would the garage people notice it?"

"No. Nobody would know it was there."

They went out and closed the doors. He put an arm round her shoulder.

"Katie," he said, "I'm tired of letting people think we're merely friends."

"So am I," she admitted.

"Then can't we have things out in the open? I want to tell everyone we're engaged, and I want to fix a date and get married. Are you ready for me to put a label on you?"

She did not hesitate.

"Yes," she said.

"Thank God." He bent and kissed her. "So should we tell your mother first?"

"Yes. She won't like it, but –"

"– but she's too wrapped up in Anvil to care as much as she would have done before he came here."

"She bought the car through him."

"She did, did she? I wonder how much he got out of it?"

Kathryn looked at him in surprise that changed to anxiety.

"You said that as if you . . . well, almost as though you didn't trust him."

"I don't have to trust him. I'm not doing any business with him."

"Is he straight, do you think?"

"I've no idea. If he's not, it's your mother's lookout. And from what I know of her, she isn't a woman who'll put herself or her money into any man's hands. So stop worrying. Have you got time to talk about where we're going to live when we're married?"

"Yes. Have you been looking round?"

"There's a flat over the shop that's going to be available in a couple of months, but I don't want to live on the job."

"I'd rather have a house than a flat."

"I know you would. Houses have gardens."

"With what I earn here, and what you make in the shop, we'll be all right for money, won't we?"

"We'll be all right anyway, money or no money."

"I wish I could think that my mother'll be pleased," Kathryn said.

"She won't be pleased," Christopher told her. "What do we care?"

Mrs. Malden's reception of the news verged on the contemptuous.

"I hope you're not expecting me to keep you both," she said.

"We don't want anything from you."

"You will before you've been married long. You'll be pushing a pram before you know where you are. This cottage is large enough for you, but it won't accommodate your bookseller husband."

Mrs. Preston took her usual gloomy view.

"Madness," she said. "To let that rich Roach get away, and pick out a fellow with nothing in his pockets – madness."

But George and Stella and Ken were wholeheartedly glad to hear the news.

"In my opinion," Ken told Christopher, "you're a lucky chap. Katie's a gem, only just one notch below Maureen."

"I agree. By the way, I've been meaning to ask you – did you ever ask Maureen if she knew anything about that car we found?"

"Yes, I did in the end – in a roundabout sort of way. She said her dad told her that the damage to the fence was done by a tractor. He said the driver said there wasn't room in the car park, so he took it round the back, and on his way out, gave the fence a beating, and not a word to Willie before driving away."

"Do you believe that?" Christopher asked.

"Maureen believes it. If they used that back path more, she might have looked down and seen the car – before it was properly hidden by the fellow who shoved it down there. But she only goes round there once in a while. She knew nothing about any missing cars. But I've still been doing some sniffing around. I got to know a lot of regular diners when I had that job as a waiter, and one of 'em was a fellow who's got a big garage up in London. Name of Quirk. Weedy-looking sort of chap, ginger moustache, head shaped a bit like an egg. Bald. He was always on his own, but he never left Crane without driving over to Willie Bolt's shop. What d'you make of that?"

"Nothing much. Perhaps he bought his groceries there."

"Groceries, my foot. Suppose this chap wanted to get rid of a car. He'd see that Willie's fence was right above that big piece of wasteland. He'd reckon it would be a good hiding place for –"

"You're imagining things."

"Maybe I'm imagining things, but I'll bet you any money there's a connection between that bloke and Willie Bolt – and between Willie Bolt and that car."

Christopher smiled.

"Let me know if you find out what it is," he said.

10

The success of the art club gave George a good deal of work. He had to refuse applicant after applicant, and he also had to phrase each refusal in as tactful a way as possible. They now had the full complement of twenty members.

Not all the pupils kept their eyes on their canvases. Miss Grail's sister had joined the group, and she made, George thought, a pleasant addition to the cast. She was a tall, willowy widow, with curves instead of Miss Grail's angles, and a soft, appealing manner quite unlike her sister's brusque approach. She was also, as Miss Grail had claimed, a good painter. While she worked, Mr. Vernon watched her, and it was obvious to all that he thought her more than charming. Soon it was known that he had asked her out to dinner. She had accepted, not only once but twice more, so the members felt that all they had to do was sit back and watch the romance develop.

It did not pursue the expected course, however. Miss Grail's sister showed no desire to do more than meet for dinner. Mr. Vernon, having much enjoyed his widower-hood, now experienced the pleasure of a courtship that exercised his tendency to gallantry, but that he could be sure was not likely to lead him into matrimony. This unde-manding companionship the club members learned to accept.

The art club, and Oliver Anvil's occupancy of the wing rooms, had completely banished Stella's feeling of loneli-ness. There was life in the house once more. Things were not quite as they had been in the past – there was less coming-and-going, fewer faces round the table at meals, no groups of young people to be seen in the garden. The only music now heard came from George's wide collection of classical cassettes. But the house had ceased to echo.

"A tenant isn't what we wanted," she told George as she was undressing for bed one night. "I'd hoped to have our grandchildren filling the house. But as it can't be that way, this is the next best thing – a nice tenant to wake the house up."

"If it makes you happy . . ."

"It's taken me back, in a way, to things as they were before the girls went away. People are still telling me we ought to move into a smaller place, but you love this house and so do I – and besides that, where would we find room to put all the things we've accumulated in the past twenty-five years?"

George, already in bed with his eyes closed, merely grunted. She turned from the dressing table to look at him anxiously.

"I've asked you this before," she said, "but I'd like to be reassured. You do like Oliver, don't you?"

"Yes." His eyes opened. "Are you beginning to have doubts about him?"

"Not exactly doubts. But he asked me whether I'd mind if he sometimes brought friends to the house, and after I'd said I didn't mind at all, I remembered that he's friendly with a lot of those people who spend their time in the bar of the hotel – not a choice crowd."

"You can hardly shut them out."

"I know that. But it isn't only Oliver who does the fraternising – Kathryn's mother goes along with him."

"You can't do anything about that, either. If he pays his rent regularly, that's all that concerns us."

"Not quite all. That first lot of friends he brought to the house sounded a bit wild. Odd, isn't it? I didn't think he'd turn out to be so . . . well, undiscriminating. I thought he was a fastidious kind of man."

"Do you want to get rid of him?"

"Heavens, no. I'm just a bit disappointed in him, that's all."

"We didn't get to know him well in Naples. Perhaps the high polish dazzled us."

"It wasn't only high polish. He was . . . what's the word for people who know a lot?"

"Erudite?"

"Yes. I can't say I took much in, but he certainly knew his history."

"You could have got most of it out of your guide book."

"I suppose so. Are *you* having second thoughts about him?"

"No. I don't think we'll have him long, somehow. He and Kathryn's mother will find a house, and my bet is that they'll move in together, wed or unwed."

"Wed," she guessed. "He's the age to settle."

"There's no such thing as a settling age." He closed his eyes. "Can I go to sleep now?"

"Yes."

His eyes opened.

"Come to think of it," he said, "I'd rather stay awake for a little while longer."

She left the dressing table and got into bed.

"Come to think of it," she said, "so would I."

On the following morning, Oliver Anvil went into the garden to look for Kathryn. Locating her in one of the greenhouses, he asked her if she was too busy to talk. She stopped working and gave him her attention.

"What can I do for you?" she enquired.

"You can tell me," he said, "what you'd think if I told you that I've become very fond of your mother. Perhaps you've noticed. Everyone else in town seems to have paired us off. But I'd like your views. You're the only relation she appears to have, and your opinion matters a great deal to me. She'll be all alone when you marry; I'd like her to marry me and live in London."

She looked at him in silence for a time. She could think of nobody who would suit her mother better as a husband – if her mother wanted a husband. He had a pleasant manner, a quietly confident air, was well informed, and well liked by almost everyone who met him.

"Has she said she'd marry you?" she asked.

"Not yet. But she hasn't said no, and she's helping me look for a house in London. It's the place we'd both prefer to live – but I'd keep a cottage here. Roach is talking about selling his. If he does, I'll buy it. Then we'll be able to come down here to see you and Hobart and George and Stella."

"I think," Kathryn said after a time, "that you're one of the few people who could make my mother happy."

"That's what I think, too. She hasn't got an easy disposition. She's not, if I might put it like this, easy to handle. But if she married me, you'd approve?"

"I don't see what difference my approving or disapproving would make, but – yes, I think you'd make a good pair."

"Thank you. When are you going to marry Hobart?"

"Not for some months. Perhaps at the end of the year."

Though no wedding date had been fixed, Christopher decided that it was time he bought an engagement ring. He and Kathryn took a day off work and went up to London to see, said Christopher, what they could find in the cheaper range of diamonds.

Lunchtime came and they had not yet decided definitely on a ring, so they interrupted their search and went to a small restaurant. From their table at the window they observed the busy scene outside. Opposite was a row of shops and a large car showroom. As they watched, a tall burly man walked into the showroom and greeted three men already standing there. Christopher's eyes went from them to the large nameplate on the door.

"Quirk's," he said. "Ken mentioned a man named Quirk

who used to go – who probably still goes – down to Crane. He must be the one leaning against that green car. Ken mentioned a garage, but said nothing about a showroom. What a fine selection of cars," he added.

"There's a lot we need before we start thinking of fancy cars," Kathryn said, interpreting him correctly. Christopher grinned in response.

"You're right. Look, I'd like to go back and take another look at that ring we nearly bought – the one with the sapphire."

They returned to the shop after lunch, and when they went back to Outercrane, it was on Kathryn's engagement finger. They went into the house to show it to George and Stella.

"It's a good buy," George told Christopher. "In a few years it'll have trebled in value, and you'll be able to sell it and buy a car like the one Katie's mother has got herself."

Stella, having admired the ring, said little. She was grappling with a problem with which she knew George could not help her: whether the arrangement they had made with Oliver Anvil had really been a wise one. He was as charming and as considerate as ever, but no day passed without his bringing friends to the wing rooms for drinks – people whose presence she was beginning to dislike. She said as much to Kathryn and Christopher now.

"It isn't that they disturb us," she said, "but we see them coming and going, and it's easy to see they've had a good deal to drink."

"As long as they don't interfere with us," George said, "I can't see that it matters."

"What matters," Stella said, "is that Oliver has friends of that kind at all. I wouldn't have said they were his type."

"And I," Christopher told Kathryn as he walked to the cottage with her, "would have said they were."

"His type?"

"Yes. He's got a hail-fellow-well-met side to him, and

that's why he likes them." He stopped. "Show me your ring again."

He dropped a kiss on to her engagement finger.

"Tell me," he asked, "why just putting a gold circle on to your finger makes you feel more mine than you were before? Perhaps it's a symbol." He took her into his arms. "Oh Kathryn, my love, I wish I had more to give you. When I say 'All my worldly goods', what do I mean? Nothing but a shop with some books in it. I'm not an envious man, but sometimes when I look at all the moneyed people in this place, I wish I had some of their worldly goods."

"I don't. With the bookshop, and my earnings, and the bit of income I've got, we'll be all right."

This failed to cheer him, and he went home in a mood of despondency. Shortly after he got back, Ken came to his rooms and spoke in a tone of excitement.

"Guess what?" he said. "There's been a car snatch."

"A what?"

"Car snatch."

"Whose?"

"Mrs. Malden's."

Christopher stared at him.

"Don't be an idiot! I've only just left Kathryn. She would have known –"

"No, she wouldn't. There hasn't been time for the news to get around. Her mother was in Crane, picking up a prescription that was being made up. She wasn't in the shop more than a few minutes, but she did her usual trick of leaving the keys in the car. Someone got in and drove off. Just like that. She came out, searched, screeched, and went to the police."

"That beautiful new car!"

"Yeah. The one she's been showing off in."

"But she only bought it –"

"That's right. In again, out again, away again."

"Where is she now?"

"At the Deepleys'. That's where she went first – after seeing the police. Funny thing – we don't get much crime here in Crane and Outercrane, so when a thing like this hits us, it hits us hard."

"Gone! That beautiful car!"

"If you ask me, gone for good. I know something about stolen cars. They get stolen for lots of reasons, but the easiest trick these car thieves go in for is making the car over and turning it into a new one. New everything – from the paint onwards. Next time you see Mrs. Malden's car, you won't know you're looking at it. They're a golden shower of opportunities, stolen cars are. They export 'em under forged papers, then sell 'em to unsuspecting buyers. I'm not sorry for Mrs. Malden. She wanted people to see her driving round in that car – and they saw her and one of 'em decided she'd been showing off for long enough. Let's see what help her friend Oliver's going to be. Where're you going?"

"Back to the cottage, to see Kathryn. Her mother'll come back in a state of . . ."

"Relax. You can't do nothing about it. Wait till the morning."

"No."

"Then I'll go with you."

They walked to the Deepleys' together. They found George and Stella and Oliver doing their best to calm the enraged Mrs. Malden. Kathryn was making coffee; she brought it in, but her mother wanted none of it. After a time, Oliver drove her away – to the hotel, he said, to meet some of their friends and try to get her into a calmer frame of mind.

"Why has she given up all hope of getting the car back again?" Stella asked when they had driven away.

"Because she knows she won't," Ken said. "Well, I'll be getting back home."

He walked out of the house with Christopher and Kathryn, who were going to the cottage.

"Come too," Kathryn invited.

"Thanks, but nope. I'll go home and brood over my own troubles."

"You've got troubles?" Christopher asked.

"Perhaps that's the wrong word. I'm just worried, that's all."

"What about?" Kathryn asked.

"It's not what, it's who. My boss. He's too cagey for my liking. He plays things too close to his chest. He keeps all his papers locked away in a leather case."

"There's nothing to worry about in that, is there?" Christopher asked.

"Yes, there is. It's not natural. Most people leave things lying around – letters, cards, odds and ends of paper. But not him. Everything's under lock and key. It might be because he doesn't trust me – after all, I was shoved at him without references – or he's keeping all his business affairs out of sight of what you might call suspicious eyes."

When he had gone, Kathryn said that perhaps the time was coming when he would lose yet another job.

"I don't think he'd mind much," Christopher said. "He's getting a bit fed up with Oliver."

They sat side by side on a sofa, her head against his shoulder. In spite of other people's troubles, life seemed to them to be good.

"If I ever left the Deepleys," she said, 'I'd like to start a small nursery garden, with Ken doing the digging. We'll need a house with some land."

"Try starting a nursery first," he counselled. "Not plants. I'd like children while we're still young." He lifted one of her hands and kissed the palm. "Do you miss me when I'm not with you?"

"Of course I do."

"I think of you every moment of the day. All the time I'm handling books, my mind's on you. Do you know what *I'd* like to do one day? I'd like to start up as a bookseller who gets hold of volumes that have gone out of print, or that have some kind of special literary value. Books that researchers need. Books that only genuine scholars can understand. If you can say I've a spark of ambition, that's what it is. Do you think there's anything in it?"

"Yes, I do."

She went with him to the door when he took his leave.

"I've just remembered," she said. "George said something yesterday about developing that waste land at the end of the garden."

"Coincidence, isn't it? It's not so long since we went down there."

"It means he'll find that abandoned car. I think he's going down to make an inspection, and if he does, he'll want me to go with him."

George's inspection indeed brought to light the car which had fallen, or been driven or pushed from the back path of Willie Bolt's shop. He walked round at once with Kathryn to enquire into the matter.

"Don't tell me you know nothing about it," he said angrily to Bolt. "You couldn't have failed to notice the damage to your fence."

"What could I do about it?" Bolt asked. His tone was aggressive, but there was no force behind his denials to George. "Some customer or other –"

"You told people the damage was done by a tractor. Well, I'm going to have the car looked at and if possible identified. You'd better have a convincing story for the police when they come round."

The car was hauled up to Bolt's drive. Identification was all but impossible, but after days of investigation by the police and enquiries made to several garage employees, it was found to have been a car stolen four months earlier from the home of a retired grocer living six miles from Crane.

"You saw it," Ken reminded Christopher. "Every single thing ripped off it, and of course, all the car papers swiped.

That's what they want most, these car thieves – the car papers."

Willie Bolt came out badly from the police investigation.

"He tried several different stories, but none of them would wash," George told Kathryn. "Ken tells me Maureen's upset."

Maureen gave her version to Stella during a hair-setting session.

"He lied, my dad did," she told her. "Barefaced, it was. Telling me it was a tractor driver. It's the only time we've ever had anything to do with the police, but there's no smoke without fire, as they say, and from now on, they're going to keep an eye on him. So am I. It shows you can't trust anybody, not even your own flesh and blood. And my dad's not the only one that's been churned up. People in the town have got nervous. I've got customers who never locked their front doors before, but there's bolts and bars going up all over the place. And shutters. People without garages are leaving their cars practically right on their front doorsteps. Ken says that crime has come to Crane."

It was about two weeks later that Christopher was surprised to see Kathryn coming into the bookshop in mid-morning. She had come on foot, was very pale, and seemed breathless.

"Anything the matter?" he asked anxiously.

"Yes. Where can we talk?"

He took her into the little room at the back of the shop and closed the door.

"What's wrong?" he asked.

"I don't know. It's just that . . ."

"That what?" He held her close to him and kissed her gently. "Tell me."

"You'll say I'm imagining things – but I'm not. I was going into Crane on my bike, but a tyre was flat and I decided to go by bus. I walked to the bus stop, and I got out at the chemist's on this corner. I was going to do some shopping and then ask you to run me home in your car. Only . . ."

"Only what?"

"Outside the chemist's, I dropped a small parcel. It rolled between the back wheels of a large car standing in the road. I bent down to pick it up, and saw . . . Chris, you're not going to believe this."

"You saw what?"

"Do you remember when my mother bought her car and I drove it into the garage that George let us have?"

"Yes, I remember."

"Do you remember something I did to the car?"

"No. Yes. You got a small scratch on a wheel hub."

"What else?"

"I remarked that the scratch looked like your initials – KM."

"Well, they're still there."

He gazed at her uncomprehendingly.

"What's still there?"

"The mark. The initials. You can't see them unless you look closely, but I was groping for this packet and I found myself staring at them. They're the same, Chris. There's no mistake. The car's quite different – it's a sort of dark grey and it doesn't look anything like my mother's car – but the mark on the wheel hub is still there."

He had opened the door of the little room.

"Come on," he said.

They hurried through the shop and on to the road. Outside the chemist's was a car, but it was not dark grey and it was not large.

"It's gone!" Kathryn spoke in despair.

"You didn't think of taking the number?"

"No. All I thought of was getting to you."

They entered the chemist's shop. It was full of people but

Christopher's enquiry as to who had owned a large grey car sounded lame and elicited no information.

"If it's around here, we'll see it again," he told Kathryn on the way back to the bookshop.

"Ken's often in town. Shall I tell him to –"

"No. This, Kathryn, is to be kept between us – you and me."

"Why?"

"Because if you're right, and if those marks are the ones you made driving into George's garage, we've hit on something that somebody wouldn't like us to know. You're not to mention this to anybody – understand?"

"Yes. Not even Ken?"

"Not even Ken. Not yet. And now I'm going to take you home."

They saw no sign of any grey car during the next weeks. George Deepley kept Kathryn busy going up and down to the undeveloped edge of the property, and Ken's free time was also spent there, helping the men who had been employed to do the clearing. But one night he walked over to talk to Christopher as he was locking up the bookshop.

"I've got something interesting to show you," he said. "But you'll have to get a move on. And you'll need your car."

In the car, he directed Christopher, to the latter's surprise, to George Deepley's drive and to the edge of the half-cleared part of the garden. He got out and went round to open Christopher's door.

"Follow me," he said, "but don't talk. This is a secret expedition." He began the descent. "Mind your clothes," he warned. "There are mantraps all over the place where they've rooted up the bushes. Now come up here."

Christopher followed him up the slope that led to Willie Bolt's property. When they had almost reached the top, Ken seized his arm.

"Now listen to me," he said in a low voice. "I told you,

didn't I, that I've never had so much as a sniff at any of Mr. Anvil's papers?"

"Yes."

"Well, there was an unstamped note shoved into the letter box this morning. My bet is that it came from Willie Bolt's shop. Take a look into that back window – but keep your head low."

Christopher pulled himself up cautiously to a point from which he could see the window of a small room overlooking the damaged fence. In the room were two men. One was Willie Bolt. The other, to his utter astonishment, was Aubrey Roach.

"See that?" Ken pulled him back. "Anvil locked that note away, as usual – but how much will you bet that it was from Bolt, to tell him Roach was coming? This isn't a weekend, so what's Roach doing here? What's he having a nice, cosy chat with Willie Bolt for? And –"

"You've no reason to connect the meeting with Mr. Anvil."

"No reason, no. Just that unstamped letter. It couldn't have been Roach who delivered it, but it could have been Willie Bolt, choosing a time when he knew Mr. Deepley was out in the garden and Mrs. Deepley out shopping."

"You've no proof that –"

"Proof, no. Just a hunch, that's all."

They turned and scrambled back to the place at which they had left the car.

"There's a tie-up somewhere," Ken said. "I'd lay money on it, if I had any. Maureen's out; her sister's serving in the shop. Roach could come and go without anyone but Willie knowing he was there. Say what you like, there's something about Roach that doesn't add up. Look at the way he led two separate lives – one here, one in London, and never the two overlapping. What puzzles me is where Anvil comes in. He and Roach aren't supposed to know each other."

"Why couldn't they have done this by phone?"

"Because I'm there to answer it, most of the time, and I know their voices – Bolt's and Roach's, both. Do you think there's something funny going on, or don't you?"

"There may be. But what the hell can you do about it?"

"I can keep my eyes and my ears open. I'm going to watch them." He took his place beside Christopher in the car. "But you know something? I don't think I'll be able to watch for long. I think Anvil's getting the idea that I'm too nosey for my own good."

11

Ken's prophecy was fulfilled the following week, when Oliver sought out George and Stella and asked if he could have a word with them.

"It's about Ken," he said.

Something in his tone told them that no good news would be forthcoming. He followed them into the drawing room and faced their apprehensive countenances.

"What about Ken?" George asked.

"Isn't he doing well?" Stella asked. "I thought he'd settled down –"

"It's not his work," Oliver said. "It's just a little matter of a pair of cuff links."

"Cuff links?" George echoed in bewilderment.

"Yes. They weren't of much value – or not excessive value – but they've gone. Nobody but Ken could have taken them."

There was a brief silence. Then Stella spoke hotly.

"I don't believe it. Ken wouldn't steal anything."

"That's my opinion too," said George. "He's got his faults, but he's no pilferer."

"I'm afraid this shows that he is," Oliver answered. "I don't need to tell you that I wouldn't have mentioned the matter if I hadn't been quite certain of my facts. There's no mistake. Perhaps it's my fault for having left the things about. To tell you the truth, I've been uneasy about small sums of money I've left lying here and there."

"We've known him," George said, "since he was a child. He's been coming into this garden, into this house, into Stella's kitchen all his life. He's never laid a finger on anything."

Oliver raised his eyebrows.

"There's always a first time," he pointed out. "And he might see some difference between stealing from old friends like yourselves, and pocketing the odd object belonging to a stranger. As I said, I'm sure of my facts. I know this is a shock to you both, but in the circumstances, I'd be grateful if you'd try and find me someone else."

"Have you said anything to him?" George asked.

"Not yet. Don't imagine for a moment," he added, "that I'm going to bring the police into this. The very fact of his dismissal will put prospective employers on their guard."

The news left Stella shattered. If Ken was dismissed, it would be impossible to prevent the news from spreading round the town. It would be talked of in Crane and Outercrane and would end his chances of getting any other work. She was certain that Oliver was mistaken – but he seemed equally certain that he was right.

For the first time, she admitted to herself that she had for some time regretted renting the wing rooms to him. She could not decide what had brought her finally to this realisation, but small things, she thought, had added up to make her wish that he had never proposed living in the house.

George was equally distressed.

"Like you," he told Stella when they were alone, "I find it hard to believe that Ken would do a thing like this. All the same, Oliver wouldn't have made the accusation unless he'd been pretty sure of what he was saying. I would have said that Ken would never take anything that didn't belong to him, but you've got to remember that he's got nothing but what he earns, and he's desperate to get enough money together to marry Maureen."

"What does Oliver know about him?" she demanded. "Nothing. We've known him all his life. He'd never –"

"That's what I think too," said George. "He'd never. All we can do is wait and see if Oliver changes his mind about sacking him."

Ken had guessed what was in the air.

"Something about a pair of cuff links," he told Christopher and Kathryn when they met in the garden early next morning. "I'm supposed to have pinched 'em. He hasn't come out into the open and said so yet, but I know he's trying to get rid of me."

Kathryn spoke in an angry tone.

"He could do that without accusing you of stealing!"

"He could, yeah. But this way, he'd reckon I'd keep my mouth shut. If I opened it, I wouldn't get another job. And if I didn't get another job, nobody'd believe anything I said against him. I knew from the first that he wasn't what he made himself out to be. If I were you, Katie, I'd keep an eye on your mother. She's got to the stage where she does what he tells her to do. It looks as though he's aiming to marry her, but perhaps she shouldn't be so sure."

This was no consolation to Kathryn, whose mother was invariably seen in the company of Oliver, and who now spoke openly of remarrying. But her worry was diverted by Christopher's next words.

"There's something Kathryn and I ought to tell you, Ken. Kathryn drove her mother's new car into the garage one day, and left a small scratch on a wheel hub. There's no mistaking the mark – it just happened to take the form of her initials – KM. A sort of zigzag, but quite clear – if you knew where to look. She saw the mark on a wheel hub again the other day – but this time, the wheel was on a large grey car."

"Where?" demanded Ken.

"Outside the chemist's, near the bookshop. She dropped a parcel, stooped to pick it up, and there was the mark. She came straight to me, but we decided to say nothing to anyone."

"You were bloody well right, man! Do you realise what this means?"

"Yes. A stolen car racket. Unfortunately we haven't seen the car again since that day."

"And you most likely won't. It means they've found a buyer. It might be anywhere . . . anybody living between Land's End and John O'Groats. You didn't get the number?"

"No. I was a fool not to, but I didn't," Kathryn admitted.

"Then what I'm going to do," Ken said, "is start nosing around again. Did the car look anything like your mother's?"

"No. But it was about the same size – very big. Otherwise . . . no, there was no resemblance."

"There wouldn't be." He turned towards the house. "I've got to go in and press the gent's pants. Watch the headlines – I'm going to be sacked for swiping those cuff links. I never saw the ones he's described, but lately he's asked me a hundred times if I know where they've gone."

He left them, and Kathryn turned to Christopher.

"I'm frightened," she said.

"There's nothing to be frightened of. We might have got ourselves mixed up with some car thieves, but don't worry – we're not in any danger."

"Everything's different." She put a hand into his. "My mother's different – she doesn't think or talk of anything but money. George is different – he's worrying about Ken. You're different – you're worrying too, though you won't admit it. Stella's different – I think she wishes she'd never let Oliver have the wing."

"You're the one who's doing the worrying," he said, and put an arm around her.

"I've just got this feeling that something's going to happen."

Nothing of any moment occurred. But an event took place two hours later which did nothing to calm Kathryn's uneasiness. She went with George and a garden designer

161

down to the newly-cleared part of the property. When the
two men left, she did some tidying up and then, on an
impulse, clambered up to see if the back room of Bolt's shop
was as clearly visible as Christopher had said it was. She
began the ascent and then, as her head came level with the
path, she stopped abruptly.

Two men were standing there – two men who it was
supposed had never met one another. One was Aubrey
Roach. The other was Oliver Anvil. Their cars were parked
close by.

Her heart beating fast, she crouched behind a bush. She
could see enough to know that some papers passed between
them. Then they walked to the cars, talking as they went,
got in and drove away.

She did a rapid calculation. There was just time before
Oliver's arrival at the house – if he was going there – for her
to telephone and tell Ken what she had seen. She used the
Deepleys' telephone – and then she got out her bicycle and
rode fast to the bookshop. Ken joined them there, bringing
the sandwiches Stella had given him for his lunch. Christopher made coffee and cut more sandwiches in the room at
the back of the bookshop. While they were eating, they
assembled the evidence.

"If you ask me," Ken said, "they're all in on it: Anvil,
Roach and Bolt. They won't be the only ones. Three's not
enough to make a gang, and car stealing needs a network.
Who does what, or when, or how, I've no idea. But I bet
there's a lot more of them."

"We're not concerned with gangs," Kathryn said. "All I
want to know is who stole my mother's car. It isn't likely
to be any of the three we know about."

"Why not?" Ken demanded. "Anvil helps her to buy it,
then he gets someone to steal it and do it over and re-sell it
as a second-hand car. Our first job is to find out who's
bought a large second-hand car – if anybody has – round
this district."

"Why this district?" Kathryn asked. "You said yourself that it might be anywhere."

"I still say so, but then again, it might be a local job. I'm going back to that garage I used to work at. Some of them know more than they admit to. Sometimes, when I was working there, I heard bits of talk that sounded suspicious, and I used to think it might be nice to be on the inside. It seemed to me such an easy racket. Someone says to the head chap 'Get me a Rolls' and out go the scouts and pick up one and make it over and share out the dough when it's sold. Nothing to it. No waiting on somebody and pressing their suits and serving 'em dinner and saying yes, sir, no, sir."

"How about the risk of ending up in prison?" Kathryn asked.

Ken gave a laugh, choked on a mouthful and waited until he could speak.

"How many of 'em end up in jug?" he asked derisively. "Just you count up the number of cars that get pinched, and compare it with the number of crooks that get put in the can for pinching 'em. Makes you laugh. And talking of police, why didn't Anvil call 'em in when he thought I'd got his cuff links?" He finished another mouthful. "It's not too late. He might still ask 'em to step in and arrest me. But somehow I don't think he will."

"Because you're a friend of the Deepleys," Kathryn said.

"That's not his reason for doing it this way. What he's doing now is pretending to think it over. Tomorrow, or the next day, he'll say to me: 'Sorry, Preston, but' . . . et cetera et cetera."

He drank his coffee and left them.

"Do you think he's right about –" Kathryn began.

Christopher broke in firmly.

"We're not going to talk any more about Ken and crooks," he said. "We're going to talk about ourselves. This evening, I'm going to take you to see a house I've found that might suit us."

"Where?" she asked.

"Two miles the other side of Crane. It wants a lot of doing up."

"How many rooms?"

"Living room, kitchen, bathroom, three bedrooms, all small, but we could knock down a wall and make one of them into a decent size. We could also fit in another bathroom."

"Is there a garden?"

"There's a lot of wild ground surrounding the house. It's ugly – the house, I mean. Nobody's lived in it since it was built twelve years ago."

"How much?"

"They're working it out. It would mean a mortgage and it would take all I've got to put up the rest of the money."

That evening, he took her to see the house. It stood alone in the middle of an area which had once been part of the grounds of a derelict mansion. This had been demolished and the grounds scheduled for a park. The house they were looking at had been intended as the park-keeper's home, but nothing had so far been done to prepare the grounds. The house had been up for sale for more than a year but had not been sold, Christopher guessed, because it was not near any public transport.

"But would they let me have a garden of my own?" Kathryn asked.

"They might even offer you the job of head gardener. Do you like it?"

"Yes. It looks awful as it is now, but just think what we can make it into."

"I'm thinking. It would be like rebuilding a Roman ruin."

"What about paying for it?"

"In instalments. Could you be happy here?"

"I'd be happy anywhere – with you. Why do you need to ask?"

"Just to get reassured now and then."

"I wonder," she said musingly, "what it'll be like to be in a real home again – a home of the kind I remember before my father died? You would have liked him. He was as different from my mother as anybody could be. Why they married, I could never understand."

"She's a very attractive woman."

"When she wants to be. They weren't happy. Even when I was very young, I could see that much. I used to wonder why he didn't answer back, or protest, when she went at him. Now I know that he'd simply got used to it, the way I did later." She looked at her watch. "It's time we left."

"What's the hurry?"

"We're dining with George and Stella – remember?"

"My God, it had gone right out of my mind."

They delayed for a little while longer, walking round and discovering more about the house and its surroundings. The view gave them particular satisfaction. In the distance was a gleam of water, where the river that flowed through Crane took a wide curve. Nearer to the house were tall trees where rooks nested. There was a disused well and neglected flower-beds which must at one time have been part of the demolished mansion's garden. There was no sound of traffic – the road that led to the house led nowhere else, and the main road was almost a mile away.

"Would you be lonely here?" Christopher asked.

"Lonely? Were you thinking it was lonely? I was thinking it was lovely. We're late. Let's go."

When they got to Riverside House, Stella had news for them.

"It's happened," she told them as George handed out pre-dinner drinks. "Oliver has sacked Ken."

"When?" Christopher asked.

"An hour ago," said George. "The funny thing is," he added, "that not only we – Stella and I – can pretty well swear that Ken didn't take that pair of cuff links, but we're

165

both equally certain that Anvil himself doesn't think he did. It looks to us like an excuse for getting rid of Ken."

"He couldn't have done it in a more cruel way," Stella said angrily. "How could a man as nice as he seemed to be do a mean thing like this? Or was he never as nice as we thought he was?"

"Bit late to ask that now," George said. "There's no hope of getting him to change his mind. I did what I could. He wouldn't even listen."

"So what's he really like, under all that polish?" Stella wondered out loud.

"No use speculating on that either," George said. He sounded resigned. Then he turned to Christopher. "How about you two?" he asked. "Got any plans for the wedding?"

They told him about the house they were hoping to buy. Stella said that she had often driven past it.

"It's a ruin," she said. "It'll take you years to do up – if you're planning to fix it yourselves."

"We certainly couldn't afford to put it into the hands of builders," Christopher said. "But if Ken's going to be back full time on your pay-roll, perhaps you'll let him spend part of his time helping Kathryn and me to get a start on the ruin. We could pay you – or him – for the number of hours he puts in." He emptied his glass and accepted George's offer of a refill. "Incidentally, I heard Ken's grandmother tell him that if he lost this job, he could get out and stay out. She sounded as though she meant it. If she turns nasty, I'll tell her that if Ken goes, I go. I don't think she'll want to lose a nice lodger like me."

The following morning, Christopher and Kathryn took Ken to see the house. He walked round it looking thoughtful.

"I'm no builder," he told them, "but I can manage a wall or two and I can splash on some plaster and lay a roof tile. Did you make it all right with Mr. Deepley?"

"Yes."

"Good. I'm a free man now – except for my job with him." He paused and spoke in a serious tone. "You know, I think there's something in the wind. Something's going on – or due to come off. I'm more and more certain that Anvil wants me out of the way. I don't know what he's up to, but I wish I could get a start finding out."

"What exactly did he say when he sacked you?" Christopher asked.

"Not much. He paid my wages and told me to get out. So Preston pushed off. Thank the Lord I'm shot of him. I couldn't have stood him for much longer. What you lot ever saw in him is more than I can figure out. Top dressing, that's all he amounts to." He paused. "There's something I have to tell you. I've found out something – who bought that car with the mark on the hub."

"Who?" Christopher asked.

"A chap called Boxwood. Lives four miles from Crane, works for a wholesale firm of furniture dealers, bought the car three weeks ago."

"Where from?" Kathryn asked.

"There was no way of finding out. I went to his house to ask him, but he was off on his holiday, he and his wife and his father-in-law – all driven away to the Continent. They went, so the neighbours said, for two weeks, so they're due back by now. So there's only one thing to do."

"What's that?" Christopher asked.

"We pay them a short visit and see what we can find out."

12

The following day, Ken came to the house looking for George and Stella.

He found them in Stella's work-room. On a table were spread some designs George had made for Stella's enamel jewellery. Both were intent and absorbed, and focussed their attention on Ken with some difficulty.

He was carrying a small briefcase. He laid it beside the designs on the table, and spoke in a hard tone neither of them had ever heard him use.

"I've come to show you something I think you ought to see," he said. "And to tell you something you ought to hear. You'd better sit down. It might take some time to explain."

They sat. He remained standing, the briefcase close to his hand.

"You both know why I was sacked by Mr. Anvil," he began. "I was sacked for stealing. I didn't steal those cuff links, or anything else belonging to him or to anybody, and I'm certain he knows I didn't. But that's not the point. The point is that I thought as he'd called me a thief, it wouldn't be a bad idea to prove he was right. So when he went out this morning, I went into the wing and I picked up this case – it's got all his letters in it." He held up the briefcase. "This is it. Exhibit A. I bet he's missed it by now, but I don't think he'll come and claim it. Because I broke it open and took a look at the letters and papers he's been hiding ever since I went to work for him. It's interesting stuff to read, and you, Mr. Deepley, will have to go through the papers and find out what I uncovered."

"I'll do nothing of the sort!" George spoke angrily.

"You've done a damn silly thing. You've put yourself into his hands. You've –"

"Maybe. But you know what they say – set a thief to catch a thief – and that's what I've done. I opened this case and I took a look. A lot of the stuff was too complicated for me to get the hang of, but you'll be able to understand it. What it all adds up to is that he isn't the rich financial wizard he claimed to be. He's up to his neck in debt. He owes money all round the place, in England and in foreign parts too. As far as I could make out from the letters from a number of banks, his assets are just about on a level with mine. He's been living on the profits he made helping other people to buy things – like Katie's mother's car, for instance. He's mixed up in the car-pinching racket. He was borrowing money from Mr. Roach – the chap he said he didn't know. I'm not inventing this, Mr. Deepley – it's all here, in this briefcase he kept so carefully locked and out of my way. And he must know by now that it's gone, because he's come back and he'll find it isn't where he left it, and he'll know where it went." He paused. "I wasn't doing this only on my own account. I'd guessed a bit of what he was and what he was up to, and I thought you and Mrs. Deepley ought to know too." He jerked his chin towards the briefcase. "Take a look," he invited George.

George made no move to take the case.

"I'm not going to look through anything," he said firmly, "until I've let Mr. Anvil know that I've got the briefcase."

"Then you'd better hurry," Ken said. "With those papers out of his hands, he's a goner, and I bet you anything he's gone."

George strode to the door.

"Come with me," he ordered.

The three went downstairs and walked to the wing. When they entered the living room, it was at once clear that Oliver Anvil had indeed gone. Every trace of his occupancy had vanished. His bedroom was in disarray, but none of his clothes or possessions were in it; the wardrobe and drawers were empty.

"Done a bunk. I told you so," said Ken. "A quick one, too. I bet it isn't the first time he's had to get out fast. You won't see him again." He turned to Stella. "I'm sorry," he went on. "I know you liked him and liked having him living in the house. But I reckon you had a right to know what sort of snake he is."

Stella drew a deep breath.

"It's . . . incredible," she said. "He was so . . ."

"He made himself pleasant all round," Ken said. "Are you going to look through those papers, Mr. Deepley?"

"Yes," said George. "But it's a job I won't enjoy. I've always thought I was good at sizing people up. I thought he was a . . . a man of integrity."

"You can't size up the con man," Ken told him firmly. "Part of his know-how is getting people to believe he's on the level."

It did not take George long to learn from the papers in the case what kind of business Oliver Anvil had been engaged in. Perhaps the greatest shock of all was to discover how much money he owed in Naples. When they had met him there, they had assumed him to be a man of culture, charming, prosperous – and kind. Now they learned that he had left a mountain of debts behind him.

"It's . . . it's impossible to believe," George said at last. "He's a . . . a . . ."

"He's a crook!" said Ken. "And the next person who ought to know it is Katie."

George went to the window. Kathryn and Christopher were pulling a small roller over the lawn.

"Will you come in here a minute?" he called to them.

When they came in, he told them of Ken's discovery. There was a long silence after he had ended. Then Kathryn spoke in a tremulous voice.

"My mother won't believe any of this. They were . . . he

had even spoken to me about their getting married. Couldn't that have been genuine – his loving her, I mean?"

"If she hadn't come in for that money of her uncle's," George said, "I'd have said yes. But it's not likely that he told her how his affairs stood."

"Do you think he borrowed money from her?"

"No. That would have given the game away," Christopher said. "Where d'you think he's gone?"

"London, I bet you," said Ken. "You can easily disappear there. And this is the time," he added, "to tell Mr. and Mrs. Deepley that we'd got close to linking him with a car-stealing racket."

"What are you talking about?" Stella asked in bewilderment.

"Anvil knew Roach," Christopher told her. "Kathryn saw them together behind Bolt's shop."

"Willie Bolt too? Are we surrounded by snakes?" George asked.

"We'll know," said Ken, "when we discover who sold a second-hand car with a wheel hub on which Katie had accidentally left a mark we can identify. We know who bought it, but he's been out of England, on a trip somewhere. He ought to be back by now, so we can get a lot of things cleared up."

"And in the meantime," George said, "somebody's got to tell Katie's mother what's happened here this morning."

There was silence. Nobody, least of all Kathryn, appeared anxious to volunteer for the task.

"Perhaps," she said, "Oliver'll go up to London and see her and . . . well, explain that he has to go away, or . . . or something."

"She's going to get a knock," George said. "Somehow, I don't think he'll disappear without letting her know where he's gone."

"And I don't know," Kathryn said in a worried tone, "how she's going to take it. If she's really hurt . . ."

"Well," Stella spoke briskly, "I'm going to make coffee for us all. Come into the kitchen."

They sat round the table drinking it. It was a silent assembly; everybody seemed to be brooding over the events of the morning. As they rose, George saw a car stop in the drive.

"Visitor," he said. "Roach. That'll be for you, Katie."

But at the door they met not only a very subdued Aubrey Roach, but also Mrs. Malden. She looked at Kathryn and spoke in an expressionless voice.

"There's no need to tell me anything about Oliver," she said. "I know it all. Aubrey told me all there is to know. He's brought me down here to get some things I left in the hotel."

Aubrey spoke.

"What your mother intends to do," he told Kathryn, "has nothing to do with me. I just brought her down here because Anvil asked me to. He also asked me to tell her what had happened. So I did."

"Yes, he talked." There was still very little expression in Mrs. Malden's voice. "He – no, Stella, I'm not staying, I'm going. A lot of what Aubrey told me was news to me, but some of it wasn't. I'm not quite the fool many people take me for. If you thought I'd found Oliver attractive, you were only half right. I was still using my eyes and my ears. I guessed he was involved in a racket of some kind."

"You didn't guess," Roach said, "that he had no assets."

"But you may have guessed," said George, "that he, or someone he knew, stole your car."

"All right. So he's a crook. Aubrey's a crook too, but Oliver was the boss."

"And where does Willie Bolt come in?" George asked Roach.

"Nowhere." Aubrey's tone was contemptuous. "He was asked to get rid of a stolen car, and he did – and got well paid for it."

172

"And Quirk?" Christopher asked.

"Oh, you've got on to Quirk as well, have you? Well, he's in this too. There's no harm in my telling you, because you've got nothing you can take to the police." He turned to Kathryn. "What you *can* do," he said, "is stop your mother from being fool enough to –"

"Nobody's going to stop me," Mrs. Malden said. "I'm going with him wherever it'll turn out to be. I need him and he needs me. I'm going to join him."

"Do you know where he is?" Kathryn asked her.

"Aubrey knows. He'll take me there. And you can stay here and go on growing primroses and weeding flower-beds and marrying booksellers to your heart's content."

"Do you mean you're just walking out like this?"

"Didn't you hear me? I said I was going to join Oliver. I don't know when you'll see me again, and I don't suppose you care much. I've never shown any talent as a mother; it's always seemed to me an overrated profession. Come on, Aubrey, let's get going." She turned at the door. "Goodbye. Have fun."

The car drove away, leaving a stunned silence behind it. It was Stella who spoke first, in a bitter tone.

"They'll go round the world," she said, "picking up strangers at hotel reception desks and making fools of them, as Oliver did of me."

"Of us both," George said.

"Did he come to Crane because we were here? Did he come just because –"

"My bet is that he came here," Ken broke in, "because Roach was already operating from here. He came to join him, but maybe he wouldn't have come if he hadn't met you in Naples and found out all he could about you first."

"Renting the wing – why should he have done that?"

"It gave him a nice, respectable background. He went over to the Spire Hotel for his bit of fun when he felt like it."

"His one bit of bad luck," Christopher said, "was letting Ken work for him. He didn't know Ken would get on to anything."

"Do you think," Kathryn asked, "that my mother can –"

"– handle him?" George nodded. "Yes, she'll be all right. Maybe they'll soon be off to Naples together, looking for another pair of suckers."

Stella spoke in an assumed voice – Anvil's.

"Forgive me," she mimicked, "but I heard the reception clerk mention your name. and I wondered if by any chance . . ."

"Yeah. It's a nice life," Ken said. "All you have to be careful about is not to trip over yourself." He turned to Christopher. "That Boxwood chap's due back," he reminded him. "How about it?"

"Let's go," Christopher said.

Mr. Boxwood was pleased to see two young men stop at his gate to admire the large grey car standing on the drive.

"No, not new," he told them in response to their query. "Looks it, doesn't she? I've just come back from a trip round France. Went like a bird, she did."

"And as comfortable as could be." A woman had come out of the house to join them. "We just glided on, smooth as smooth."

Christopher bent down to make a swift inspection of a back wheel.

"She's certainly a beauty," Ken said. "Would it be nosey to ask where you bought her?"

"It wouldn't be nosey at all. My name's Boxwood, by the way. This is my wife."

"I'm Ken Preston and this is Chris Hobart."

"Nice to meet you. You're not the first people who've stopped to look at the car."

"Did you buy it in London?" Christopher asked.

"No. Just outside. From a garage we've dealt with for years. I was after a second-hand car and I was prepared to

174

pay for a good one. They told me they'd heard that this one was on the market, and the moment they took me out in her, I knew she was the one for me."

"Which garage?" Ken asked.

"Birdwood's, it's called. A mile or two from here, straight along this road. They're good people – at least, they've always done me well."

Christopher and Ken drove away and stopped at the Birdwood garage. There were two men working there, but only one of them knew anything about the grey car.

"I remember it well," he said. "The boss brought it over to show it to Mr. Boxwood."

"Over from where?" Christopher asked.

"I can't tell you – but it'll be written down somewhere in the office. If you're not in a hurry, I'll go and take a look."

They were not in a hurry. The man went to the small, somewhat grimy office and returned holding a paper.

"Here it is," he said. "I've written it down for you."

There were only five words on the piece of paper: Quirk's Garage, Camber Lane, London.

"Thanks," said Christopher, motioning Ken back to his car. Once safely inside, Ken drew a deep breath. "So now we know," he said. He turned to face Christopher. "What do we do next?"

"Nothing," Christopher said.

Ken's voice was high with shock.

"*Nothing?*" he echoed.

"That's right. Nothing."

"But look, man, we've found some car thieves. Are you going to let them go on operating?"

"All we've done," Christopher said, "is flush out a number of shady characters."

"All right. So we can tell the police that, can't we?"

"We can – but we won't. To bring Anvil into this means involving Katie's mother – so that's out. Roach isn't likely to show his face here again. Willie Bolt will get a fright,

175

mend his fence and mind his own business. Quirk will vanish, just like Roach."

"But –"

"We've stopped up a rat hole. We know what we know. Roach was right when he said we had nothing we could take to the police."

"Then . . . then you're just going to do a fat lot of nothing?"

"Exactly," said Christopher.

13

The following week, Aubrey Roach's property, Pond Cottage, was put up for auction. It was a fine afternoon, and George told Stella that it would be interesting to see how much it fetched.

"Not as much as he gave for it," she guessed. "He never did a thing to it except open it up for weekends."

"I think I'll go and watch the proceedings."

He was absent for some hours. When he returned, he spent some time in the garden. Stella, glancing out, saw him seated on a bench staring into space, and went outside into the garden to join him.

"You look like one of those Buddhas," she told him. "The contemplative one."

"Do I? I was just coming inside."

"Well, don't. It's lovely out here. Have you ever seen this garden looking more beautiful?"

"No. That girl Katie's a treasure."

"Is that what you were thinking about just now?"

"No. I was thinking about the auction."

"Oh, the auction? Who bought the cottage?"

There was a brief silence. A butterfly flew past, settled on a pink rose and then fluttered out of sight.

"Well, who bought the cottage?" Stella repeated. "Anyone we know?"

"Yes."

"Really? Who bought it?"

"I did," said George.

After a bewildered moment, she swung round to face him.

"You're joking, of course," she said.

"No joke. I bought it."

"But . . . but what in the world *for?*"

"For Ken and Maureen."

"For –"

"That's right. Ken and Maureen. It's time they got married. In fact, if you study her figure, you'll know it's past time. So they'll need a home."

"I see. So you thought it your duty to provide one."

"Not duty. Privilege."

"Forgive me. Privilege. What makes you think that Willie Bolt won't stop his daughter from marrying Ken?"

"I'm damn sure he can't. When he looks at his daughter's figure, he'll put up the banns. Incidentally, he's mended his fence. That means that he knows that Ken knows he's been playing around with crooks. I wouldn't be surprised if Ken didn't get some money out of him for furniture."

"To put into the cottage. Are you thinking of giving it to him?"

"Of course not. Renting. I'm going to become one of those grasping landlords. Thinking about the two of them at the auction – Ken and Maureen – it struck me that neither of them had ever had a real break. Ken, with his grousing grandmother, and Maureen with her obstructive father."

"So you bought the cottage. How much did it cost you?"

"Do we have to go into that now?"

"That means you're scared to tell me. Will they make good tenants?"

"Time alone," said George, "will tell."

At the end of the month, the art club held its first exhibition in the hall that Mr. Vernon had hired for his poetry reading. It drew a large crowd, and several pictures were sold: Miss Grail's 'Landscape by Moonlight', her sister's 'Lily Pond', three of Miss Minter's miniatures and two of Mr. Vernon's views of the river.

Displayed on a table in a corner were the results of Stella's labours – three bracelets and two necklaces in enamel work. To these Mrs. Woodley added a small enamel snuff box, and a brooch. Mrs. Truedom undertook to superintend the sales, if any, and soon reported to Stella that every item had been sold.

"Thirty pounds the lot – not bad," she said.

"Thirty pounds together with Mrs. Woodley's exhibits?" Stella asked.

"No, no, no. She got eighteen pounds, which I've handed over to her. This money's yours."

"Not mine. The starving poor's. Thank you for doing the selling."

The occasion was pronounced an unqualified success. Only Miss Minter, in spite of her sales, seemed out of spirits. It puzzled and worried Stella, but she had almost forgotten about it when, at the end of the week, Miss Minter appeared at the door of her work-room asking if Stella could spare a few minutes.

"Of course. Sit down," Stella said. "What can I do for you?" She studied the other woman for a few moments. "You know, you look a little tired. George thinks that perhaps you need a tonic. He's even prepared to recommend one."

"Tonic? No, oh no, thank you. I'm perfectly well."

"I do wish you'd let him fetch you for the lessons, and take you back afterwards."

"Thank you, no. I wouldn't dream of it. So kind of him to offer, but I really . . ."

She stopped and Stella, to her dismay, saw tears in her eyes. She drew her chair closer and put out an impulsive hand.

"Tell me what's wrong," she said. "Friends can sometimes help."

"I know. But there's really nothing, nothing at all you can do. It's just –"

"Just what?"

"It's just that I'm afraid I shall have to give up coming to the classes."

There was a pause.

"Why?" Stella enquired, and wondered whether the fees were a difficulty. She had fixed them with the Minters' modest income in mind. She could hardly offer to waive them or to pay them, for fear of giving pain or even offence. But Miss Minter's next words cleared up the dilemma.

"I'm afraid," she said, "that it's becoming – in fact has already become – impossible to leave my mother alone for such long periods."

"Isn't she well?"

Miss Minter wiped her eyes, mopped delicately at her nose and shook her head.

"She's not ill. But she's failing, and she can do less and less for herself – and when she's alone, she . . . well, she mopes."

"Has she stopped making dolls' clothes?"

"Not entirely. She sews them while I'm with her, but when I go home after having been out, I find the dresses lying where they were, untouched."

"You have to leave her to go shopping, don't you?"

"No, not any more. Mrs. Truedom does our shopping for us. She charges very little because she says she has to pass our house several times a day, so it's not out of her way."

"But you must get out of the house sometimes, for air, for exercise."

"I go for very short walks. I tell my mother where I'm going, and she sits at a window watching for me to return. But coming to the lessons means that I'm out for quite a long time."

Stella was silent. She knew it was no use suggesting domestic help. In recent years, many women in the town had answered Miss Minter's advertisements for a part-time

180

companion for an old lady. None of them had stayed long; the pay was low and Mrs. Minter was exigent, obstinate and censorious. The arrangements had broken down almost as soon as made.

"Won't you let George fetch you and take you home?" she asked. "That would lessen the time you spent away from your mother."

Once more Miss Minter shook her head.

"I wouldn't feel easy," she said. "I wouldn't be happy leaving her, and I wouldn't be happy putting George to such trouble."

There seemed nothing more to say. Reluctantly, Stella accepted her decision to give up the lessons.

"It's a wicked shame," she told George indignantly.

George looked surprised.

"The old lady can't help it, can she?" he asked. "I mean, the old get more demanding as they get older. If you remember, they tried to get a companion, but it didn't work."

"I know it didn't. So now what? Does poor little Ruth Minter have to be more and more housebound?"

"Perhaps the old lady will soon pack it in," George said, and tried without success to keep a note of hope out of his voice. "She's – how old?"

"She's ninety-two. I don't think she'll 'pack it in', as you so elegantly phrase it, until she's a hundred and two. Can't you think of something we can do?"

"Off-hand, no."

"You're a big help."

Miss Minter was not at the next lesson. Mr. Ross waited until the end of the session before making any comment. When all the other pupils had left, he addressed Stella.

"The little lady – she did not come."

"No. She –"

"She is sick?"

"No. But I don't think she'll be coming any more."

"And why so?" demanded Mr. Ross.

"She finds it impossible to leave her mother, who's very old. My husband would be only too happy to pick her up for the lessons, and take her back, but she feels that she must give up coming, as her mother frets if she's away for any length of time."

"She is not sorry to give up the lessons?"

"She's very sorry indeed."

"How old is this mother?"

"She's ninety-two. Miss Minter tried to get a sort of companion for her, but it didn't work – her mother is rather a difficult old lady."

"Where is her residence?"

"At the end of the town – one of those small houses near the river."

He said no more. The next lesson went on without Miss Minter, but at the end of it, Mr. Ross again approached Stella and spoke in a tone that was more a demand than a request.

"Please. Accompany me."

Mystified, she accompanied him down the stairs. He reached the hall, turned and gave a gesture indicating that she was still to follow him. A moment later, she found to her amazement that they were in the living room of the wing.

"These rooms –" he waved a hand, "are not a part of the house that you live in?"

"No. When my daughters were at home, they –"

"But now the rooms are empty?"

"Yes."

"In Russia, in here would be two families. Three. Perhaps even four."

"Yes, but –"

"They will remain empty?"

"I suppose so."

"The gentleman who was here – he is gone?"

"Yes."

"He will not return?"

"No."

"Then the little lady and her mother – why should they not come?"

She stared at him. It was some moments before she could speak.

"You . . . you mean . . ." she stammered at last.

"Why should they not come?" he repeated. "So, they will be close together, mother and daughter. There will only be going upstairs to the lessons. The old mother will not be alone for a long time. Have you any objection to such an arrangement?"

"I – well, I hardly . . ."

He was at the door, waiting for her to precede him.

"You will of course wish to inform your husband. But I, for myself" – he was at the front door, preparing to depart – "I myself see nothing to prevent them from coming here."

She was left in the hall, staring at his vanishing figure. Bemused, she went to the library to talk to George.

"You look pink," he commented. "Been running?"

"No. I just – could I have a drink?"

"Surely."

"I need one."

He went to a cupboard and poured out two glasses of sherry.

"This strong enough?" he enquired.

"It'll do."

"Good. Now tell me what made you pink."

"Mr. Ross. He led me into the wing living room and in the calmest possible voice made an astounding proposal."

"He wants to live there?"

"No. He wants the Minters – mother and daughter – to live there."

She was glad to see that this made George, as it had made

her earlier, a little breathless. When he could speak, he uttered only four words.

"Well, I'll be damned!"

"That makes two of us. He said I'd want to talk to you about it."

George seemed in no hurry to say any more. He had finished his drink and refilled his glass before she heard his voice.

"Well, perhaps it is," he said.

"Perhaps it is what?"

"Perhaps it's the easiest solution to get Miss Minter back to the lessons."

She put down her glass.

"Do you know what you're saying?" she demanded.

"I think so. Two old ladies need a home."

"These two old ladies have got a home."

"Only half a home, and cramped at that. They'd fit nicely into those wing rooms."

She drew a deep breath.

"I'm dreaming this," she decided. "I thought you'd take off when I told you."

He took her empty glass from her and refilled it.

"The scheme," he said in a slow, reflective voice, "has certain advantages."

"For the two old ladies, yes, certainly."

"They get more space, they look out on greenery instead of on to a concrete backyard – and the older lady need never be lonely again."

"The older lady is ninety-two. Suppose she falls ill?"

"We have an excellent doctor – and the younger lady can do the nursing, if necessary with some professional help."

"You're actually . . . you're actually saying that –"

"I'm putting before you the pros and cons."

"Never mind the pros and cons. You're actually *considering* the proposal?"

"Have you," he asked, "anything against it?"

"Yes."

"As, for instance?"

"We tried letting the wing and it was a disaster."

"Quite so. But if the tenants are two quiet old ladies we've known for over twenty years and who have been good friends of ours – there's a difference, surely?"

"Are you saying that you *agree* to let them live in the wing?"

"What I'm trying to say is that now the idea has been presented to me, I would feel very mean indeed if I didn't examine it carefully."

"You'd actually give up the wing for ever? Because that's what it would probably mean. The older lady would die, but the younger lady would be left."

"But left close to her friends. Close to her cherished paintings." He came over and took her hands. "What," he asked gently, "are your views?"

"I haven't got any. My head's swimming."

"That's the sherry. Have you anything against the arrangement?"

"*You* don't seem to have."

"I wouldn't have thought of it myself – not in a thousand years. But since it's come up, I don't see anything against it."

"You realise it'll mean they'll be there permanently?"

"Yes. I wouldn't have agreed to it – as I wouldn't have agreed when Anvil proposed living there – if there was any risk of their being within sight. But they'll be entirely on their own – and they won't bring in noisy friends, as Anvil did."

"Have you any other plans for providing housing for people – besides Ken and Maureen and the Minters?"

"None."

"What rent are you going to charge Miss Minter?"

"The same as they pay for that biscuit box they've been living in."

185

"But when one or other of the girls come home – and they're bound to come one day, even if it's only for a short holiday – they'll want –"

"They can take over the bedrooms you kept for them." He paused and then voiced a question. "When I planned this house, what made me think it was only for ourselves?"

She put her arms round him and rested her head on his shoulder.

"When you're dead, that's to say when you've 'packed it in' the town will put up a statue."

"To me?"

"To generous George Deepley. Kiss me."

"Here and now?"

"Why not?"

"Because I can think of a better place. Accompany me."

Ken came into the house with Kathryn before starting work in the garden on the following day.

"News," he told Stella. "Where's Mr. Deepley?"

When George appeared, Ken amplified.

"It's about Mr. Anvil and Mrs. Malden," he said.

"Not bad news?" George asked anxiously.

"Nope. Just news."

"They're in Singapore," Kathryn said. "A postcard came by this morning's post."

"Singapore?" Stella sounded puzzled. "Why did they have to go so far?"

"To find the sunshine," George told her. "English couple living comfortably –"

"– on my mother's money, I suppose," Kathryn said. "But I'm glad to know where they are. I was worrying."

"You needn't have worried," Stella told her. "They'll be all right until Oliver's charm wears thin. They'll be fine while he can go up to somebody and say" – her voice changed

– "Forgive me, but didn't I hear the reception clerk mention your name?"

George laughed.

"You'll never forget that, will you?" he said.

"Never," she said.